WILDSIDE PRESS MAGAZINES

Publisher
John Gregory Betancourt

**General Manager
& Creative Director**
Stephen H. Segal

H.P. LOVECRAFT'S MAGAZINE OF HORROR

Editor
Marvin Kaye

Contributing Editors
Peter Cannon
Craig Shaw Gardner
Darrell Schweitzer

H.P. Lovecraft's Magazine of Horror™ is published two times a year by Wildside Press LLC. Postmaster & others: send change of address and other subscription matters to Wildside Press LLC, 9710 Traville Gateway Drive #234, Rockville, MD 20850-7308. Single copies: $7.95 (magazine edition) or $18.95 (book paper edition), postage paid in the U.S.A. Add $2.00 per copy for shipping elsewhere. Subscriptions: four issues for $19.95 in the U.S.A. and its possessions, $29.95 in Canada, and $39.95 elsewhere. All payments must be in U.S. funds and drawn on a U.S. financial institution. If you wish to use PayPal to pay for your subscription, email your payment to: *wildside@sff.net.* The publisher may be contacted at:

Wildside Press
Attn: HPL Magazine
9710 Traville Gateway Drive #234
Rockville, MD 20850-7308
www.wildsidepress.com

Writers and artists: Please query us at *lovecraft@wildsidepress.com* prior to submitting any materials. We invite letters of comment, and we assume all letters received are intended for publication (unless marked "Do Not Publish") and become the property of Wildside Press.

Cover art by Peter Mihaichuk

H.P. Lovecraft's

MAGAZINE OF HORROR

SPRING · SUMMER 2007

Of No Cosmic Significance

Indescribable Events

That Which Does Not Die

THE OUTSIDER

editorial by Marvin Kaye

Happy Deathday

H.P. Lovecraft died on March 15, 1937, which is a little less than a year before I was born. And since I'm writing this editorial on February 15, 2007, I am just a month away from the 70th anniversary of H.P.L.'s death — so consider this issue of *H. P. Lovecraft's Magazine of Horror* our namesake's Deathday party. He left behind a vast literature of fiction, nonfiction, and letters; except for Edgar Allan Poe, perhaps no other single writer has had such a profound impact on 20th-century and contemporary fantasy literature, especially in America and England.

Up to now, this magazine has featured H.P.L.-related nonfiction in every issue, from Peter Cannon's Lovecraft-in-culture column "Unspeakable Occurrences" to Greg Lamberson's feature on movies inspired by the master's tales. We've also — alongside lots of original horror stories of all kinds — regularly presented new fiction that's chock full of Lovecraftiness, such as last issue's "The Paramount Importance of Pictures," a juicy Cthulhu-in-Hollywood tale by Lynne Jamneck.

One of our readers recently wrote, however, to say he was a bit disappointed that our last issue did not have anything written by Lovecraft himself. It's true, I have not considered it necessary to include something by the master every time out, and for two reasons: 1. We try not to run more than one reprinted piece in any issue; last time, that was Earl Godwin's masterful terror tale, "Daddy." 2. Lovecraft's best work is well known and readily available at any well-stocked book store.

Still, we want our readers to be pleased with every issue of *H.P. Lovecraft's Magazine of Horror,* so if you'd like to see more of H.P.L.'s own words in these pages, please let us know! You can email us at lovecraft@wildsidepress.com, or drop us a note at Wildside Press, attn: Lovecraft's Magazine, 9710 Traville Gateway Drive #234, Rockville MD 20850.

One of the more difficult decisions I face when we're planning the contents of each issue is what percentage of truly horrific material to include — versus stories based in the horror tradition that are nonetheless sly, parodic, or even out-and-out funny. I love the latter kind of fiction, as I know many of you do, and so we strive to offer a mix of both the darkest darkness and also the somewhat lighter darkness. Comedy isn't the only variant commodity, either: Some stories we run are sad, some contemplative, and some suffused with a strange, ethereal beauty.

On balance, I'd say the earlier issues of *H.P. Lovecraft's Magazine of Horror* have leaned more toward the fearful side of the equation. The current issue does, too, in terms of total story count — but the longest single story in this issue, as well as one of the best, is Esther Friesner's "The Really Big Sleep," which cross-matches H.P. Lovecraft with the noir detective stylings of Dashiell Hammett (or perhaps Raymond Chandler) to hilarious effect. The only other time I've seen this kind of story done so well was Charles Beaumont's "The Last Caper," which somehow managed to successfully wed the styles of Mickey Spillane and Ray Bradbury.

And humor with more than a touch of urbanity exists in Ron Goulart's "The Problem of the Missing Werewolf," a new Harry Challenge adventure. >>

> **When it comes to planning what percentage of truly horrific fiction to publish, we strive to offer both the darkest darkness and also the somewhat lighter darkness.**

>> For those readers not familiar with Harry, he's an American detective living overseas who handles cases with strong supernatural elements — often assisted by his friend, The Great Lorenzo, a stage magician whose powers tip over into real magic. Till now, Harry has only appeared in two novels, *The Prisoner of Blackwood Castle* (1984) and *The Curse of the Obelisk* (1987). I'm very pleased that Ron has agreed to bring back Harry Challenge, and not only in this story — he has already sent us two more, which readers will see over the course of the next several issues.

In my "copious spare time," to borrow Tom Lehrer's well-worn phrase, I caught two very interesting new horror-fantasy films over the past few weeks.

The Messengers is one of that seldom-successful breed, a haunted-house film in full color. Though to be precise, this one begins with an intense black-and-white flashback prologue before segueing to the present day, in which a dysfunctional couple (played by Dylan McDermott and Penelope Ann Miller) and their children have moved to a remote farmstead to hide their family shame and struggle with problems both social and economic. Problem is, the farm is quite nastily haunted — and for much of the film, only the two children are the targets, which provides for dramatic irony most deliciously tormenting. Performances and directing alike are excellent; *The Messengers* offers some original twists on what makes us shudder.

The other film, *Urchin*, though often bloody and violent, is not so much a horror film as a nightmarish urban fantasy. It's set in a depressingly grungy underground world: the New York of losers, mad dreamers, and criminal opportunists. I didn't think it was going to be to my taste, but about twenty minutes in, I asked myself, "If you don't like it, how come you're still watching?" The simple answer: I found it impossible to turn away. Writer/director John Harlacher has a potent imagination, investing his *cauchemar* with flashes of compassion and poignancy. *Urchin*'s redemptive outcome is both unexpected and surprisingly moving, in a way that reminded me of the odd little science-fiction film *Pi. Urchin* is thoroughly different in style and texture from *Pi*, but provides a similarly intense, riveting experience — I just couldn't stop watching either.

In that, it's rather like reading Lovecraft. Not in the details — but in the spirit. And so to that spirit, again, I say: Happy Deathday, H.P. ⏣

book reviews ✳ by Craig Shaw Gardner

Vampires, Grim and Goofy

So let's talk about vampires. *Again?* I hear you say. *Aren't you always talking about vampires?* Ah, but this is different. I'm talking the Big Honking Vampire Novel, here. Not to be confused with the romantic vampire novel, the detective vampire novel, the funny vampire novel, etc. I'm talking about one of those occasional vampire novels that attempts to redefine those bloodsuckers and give us a fun ride along the way. For point of reference, think *They Thirst* by Robert McCammon. Now that's a Big Honking Vampire Novel.

This time around, I'm talking about **Jim Moore**'s **Blood Red**. Big cast of characters, mysterious stranger coming to town, neat setting in a fictitious town that bears a strong resemblance to Newport, R.I. Jim Moore always writes a good yarn, with entertaining characters, and *Blood Red* is no exception.

I had high expectations for this sucker. I was really hoping this would be Moore's big breakout book. But the book contains a near-fatal flaw.

A warning here: For those who don't want any plot points spoiled, skip down another half dozen paragraphs. Everybody else proceeds at their own risk.

Blood Red contains a number of nifty ideas in its reinvention of vampire myth. First among these is the thing our vampire fears most — the blinding light of pure faith.

So, to rid himself of this problem, our bloodsucker hires a local call girl to seduce every priest, rabbi, and minister in town. Which she promptly does, without any difficulty whatsoever. And all the rabbis, ministers, and priests hide in shame for the rest of the plot.

Sigh. How shall I list the plot problems here? Let's number them, shall we?

One: That "blinding light of faith" idea is brilliant — but then Moore cuts himself off at the knees by not using it at all. Wouldn't there be other individuals in town beyond the ministry with a faith strong enough to stand up to the vampires? Or perhaps, even better, Moore could have shown, say, a damaged priest try to go up against the vampire anyway and fail, giving the concept a personal dimension. Moore does the equivalent here of showing us the loaded gun on the first page and then never using it, which ends up being very dissatisfying, at least to this reader.

BLOOD RED by Jim Moore (Earthling Publicatons, limited edition hardcover, $40)

GIL'S ALL FRIGHT DINER by A. Lee Martinez (Tor, trade paperback, $12.95)

THE EYES OF THE CARP by T.M. Wright (Cemetery Dance Publications, limited edition hardcover, $30)

Two: The ease with which our young call girl mows down the local religious leaders is simply not believeable. Any novel with a strong fantasy element needs to be logically consistent in order to maintain its credibility. Surely, some members of the ministry might be weak. We've seen it in the headlines. But every single one of them? Now, if this call girl had some special power of her own, a "talent" that made her irresistible, which the vampire recognized, well, I'd still find it far-fetched, but I'd accept the explanation. But without this, I found myself looking at the author pulling the strings rather than watching the characters make believable choices.

Moore features other characters with interesting "talents" as a part of their personality — another one of the protagonists, for instance, is a talented computer hacker who seems able to destroy anyone's credit rating in a few keystrokes, and the two main cops have the kind of aim and firepower that would overwhelm any Italian Zombie Flick. It makes for fun characters, but none of the "talents" really advance the plot, so much as sort of "go along for the ride."

It's too bad, really. Moore obviously wanted to attack the vampire book from an entirely new direction, and in many ways he succeeds (Later on in the book, there's a moment with crows, of all things, that I thought was flat-out brilliant.) If you want your vampire books to be big and action packed, you'll still find a lot to like in *Blood Red*. It's a good read, but it falls just short of being a great one.

Gil's All Fright Diner, by A. Lee Martinez, has a vampire, too. And a werewolf. Who happen to be named Duke and Earl. Earl's the vampire. He has a comb-over. And a problem meeting women.

Werewolf Duke and Vampire Earl are the good guys. And their nemesis is a high school cheerleader-type named Tammy, though she prefers it if you call her Mistress Lilith, the Queen of the Night.

As you can no doubt tell by now, we're back in funny vampire territory. Not to mention funny zombie territory, and, as the book progresses, we hit funny elder gods/end of the world territory. And did I mention that all of this takes place in Texas? Of course it does.

This is a horror comedy for horror fans, and Martinez makes his werewolf and vampre protagonists quite sympathetic. The book manages to be funny while playing fair with genre conventions, much like the horror film comedy *Shaun of the Dead* fully respected the conventions of the zombie flim. I don't want to give away any more of the jokes, but if you liked my description above, you'll like *Gil's All Fright Diner*. It's the sort of book that doesn't go for the big brass ring (a la *Blood Red*) but is still consistently entertaining.

Tons of stuff — good stuff — is coming out from the small press. You'll find a lot of first rate short-story collections coming out from Cemetery Dance, Borderlands Press, P.S. Publishing, Earthling Press, and half a dozen other high-quality houses. Many of these presses also give us limited editions of new books that have a mass-market printing elsewhere, or will release first hardcover editions of quality horror fiction that has only been released in paperback form. And, from the proliferation of such small ventures, business appears to be thriving.

Borderlands is trying their hand at well-produced audiobooks (the *Dark Voices* series — the first one, Thomas F. Montelone's *Horn of Plenty* is wonderfully entertaining). Cemetery Dance is exploring the graphic-novel field. I've seen some pages for an upcoming Glenn Chadbourne/Stephen King project that are simply amazing. But perhaps the most exciting development is that a number of small-press publishers have begun novella programs.

For years, the novella was sort of the "odd length out" in fantastic fiction. Running 20,000 words or more, these pieces were too long for all but a select few to be printed in genre magazines, but they were usually too short to be printed as stand-alone mass-market books. Yet the novella often seems the perfect length to tell the fantastic tale, and many of the most notable sf, fantasy, and horror stories, from Michael Moorcock's "Behold the Man" to Stephen King's "The Body," are that in-between, novella length.

Now a number of small press houses are publishing these shorter works, and I hope they can find an audience. From the first couple of novella-length books I've read from these publishers, I think they're on to something good.

First up is **T.M. Wright**'s **The Eyes of the Carp**, part of a very classy set of limited hardcover novellas Cemetery Dance has been putting out the last couple of years. I'm a big fan of Wright's. I like the way he gets inside his characters, and lets the stream-of-con-

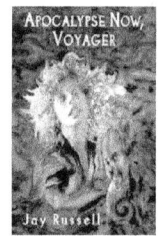

APOCALYPSE NOW, VOYAGER
by Jay Russell
(Earthling Publications, limited edition trade paperback, $14)

WE3 by Grant Morrison & Frank Quitely (Vertigo, trade paperback, $13.95)

THE ILLUSTRATED STEPHEN KING TRIVIA BOOK
by Brian Freeman and Bev Vincent / illustrated by Glenn Chadbourne (Cemetery Dance Publicatons, trade paperback, $20)

ciousness of their thoughts add to the horror. He usually mixes these sometimes surreal passages with other characters, more grounded in normality, or other more "real" events. Not here. From the first page of *Carp*, I realized I was in the hands of an unreliable narrator, lost not just to reality but in some places to time and space. We're in deep psychological territory here. The book *Carp* most reminded me of was Jim Thompson's *A Hell of a Woman*. The book lasts just long enough, and leaves the reader with a real sense of unease. This isn't the place to start with T.M. Wright, but if you've liked his more mainstream books, chances are you'll like this, too.

The next novella is a different kettle of fish entirely. **Apocalypse Now, Voyager**, is a novella featuring **Jay Russell**'s recurring protagonist Marty Burns, former child star and Hollywood detective. (Burns has previously appeared in the novels *Celestial Dogs* and *Burning Bright*.) The book takes place in a mythical Los Angeles, full of all sorts of weird characters — like the people who have decided to become dogs by gluing fur all over their bodies — and Marty's quest up the dry Los Angeles River bed with a naked dead woman in a shopping cart. But all is not as it seems. *Voyager* is a wonderfully screwy fantasy with horror and Hollywood (see the title) overtones, and Earthling has given us a very nice paperback edition. This was the first time I've encountered Marty Burns — but now that I have, I've got to go back and find the others.

A couple of quick mentions to round out the column:

The Vertigo line of comics, home of *Sandman* and *Preacher*, has consistently given us cutting-edge graphic work. If you're looking for something different, may I recommend **We3**, with story by **Grant Morrison** and art by **Frank Quitely**. It's a story about genetic experiments gone horribly wrong. More specifically, it's a story of cute family pets as killing machines. It's definitely horror of a different sort.

Do you know your Stephen King? Do you eat, breathe, and live the books written by the modern horror master? If so, **The Illustrated Stephen King Trivia Book** is up your alley. This very nicely produced, over 400-page (!) tome asks every obscure question you could possibly imagine about King. I could hardly answer any of them, but certain people who read this column will need the book immediately. You know who you are. 🎧

"But are not the dreams of poets and the tales of travellers notoriously false?"

— H.P. Lovecraft

Kudos for Cthulhu

Lovecraftians who may have wondered if there was a link between the Providence Gentleman's fiction and Erich von Däniken's *Chariots of the Gods?* and other books claiming that aliens visited Earth in ages past will find Jason Colavito makes a convincing case in his highly readable study from Prometheus Books, *The Cult of Alien Gods: H.P. Lovecraft and Extraterrestrial Pop Culture.*

Colavito argues that the Armed Forces editions of H.P.L.'s works had an important influence on postwar French culture — in particular, on two mystically-inclined individuals: Jacques Bergier, who translated Lovecraft into French in the 1950s, and his pal, Louis Pauwles, coauthor (with Bergier) of *Morning of the Magicians*, a chronicle of ancient mysteries. *Morning of the Magicians* helped spawn books by Robert Charroux that expanded on the ancient-astronaut theme. In the 1960s, two of Charroux's books fell into the hands of von Däniken, a Swiss hotel clerk, who would soon launch a lucrative new career as an author, starting with *Chariots of the Gods?*, published in the U.S. in 1971. As background, Colavito not only accurately surveys Lovecraft's life and writing career but also charts the evolution of H.P.L.'s posthumous fame up to the present. He even quotes from the Library of America *H.P. Lovecraft: Tales* edited by Peter Straub, though oddly he doesn't use S.T. Joshi's Penguin editions when citing stories not included in that omnibus volume.

One contemporary French writer who appreciates Lovecraft (at a more sophisticated level than Bergier or Pauwles) is Michel Houellebecq, whose 1991 meditation, *H.P. Lovecraft: Against the World, Against Life*, is now available in English translation from Believer Books. The bestselling author of such controversial novels as *The Platform and The Possibility of an Island*, Houellebecq shares with H.P.L. a cynical worldview. In his preface, written in 1998, Houellebecq remarks that Lovecraft's "originality appears to me greater today than ever." He goes on to say of H.P.L.'s style: "His writing in fact is not implemented entirely through hypertrophies and delirium; there is also at times a delicacy in his work, a luminous depth that is altogether rare." By example, he cites a lyrical passage from "The Whisperer in Darkness" describing the narrator's entry into Vermont. Filling out what would otherwise be a slim volume are "The

"There is at times a delicacy in his work, a luminous depth that is altogether rare."

~ Michel Houellebecq on H.P.L.

Whisperer in Darkness" and "The Call of Cthulhu," two of what Houellebecq calls the "great texts." Stephen King provides an insightful introduction, though one can only hope that the editors in any reprint will correct two errors: that H.P.L. influenced William Hope Hodgson, who died in World War I; and that publisher Arkham House is no more.

In an essay entitled "The Heroic Nerd" in the Oct. 19, 2006, issue of *The New York Review of Books*, critic Luc Sante, a Belgian by birth, disputes a couple of points raised in Houellebecq's book, but mainly offers a distorted view à la L. Sprague de Camp, the prose equivalent of the David Levine caricature of H.P.L. that first ran in the Oct. 31, 1996, issue of the *New York Review* (to illustrate Joyce Carol Oates's sympathetic piece tied into S. T. Joshi's *Lovecraft: A Life*). That Lovecraft should receive attention in one of America's leading intellectual journals is of course an honor (the Library of America *Tales* is nominally the other recent work under discussion), though one wishes that an editor might have caught such basic errors as the following: "he assumed the archetype of the nineteenth-century man of letters" (wouldn't "eighteenth-century" have been more appropriate?); "he was only forty-seven when he died" (did Sante consult an old Arkham House edition edited by August Derleth?); "he really did suffer from his fear of cold" (no, low temperatures themselves caused him to suffer, not his fear of them).

While Sante gets the broad strokes right, he evidently hasn't read his Joshi — or any informed commentator on Lovecraft of the last few decades. In a footnote, he concedes that the Arkham House *Selected Letters* volumes reveal a more interesting human being than the horror fiction, but he prefers to dwell on H.P.L. as misfit, racist, and dubious stylist. Most provocatively, Sante asserts, "The stories 'He' and 'The Horror at Red Hook' make it sound as though he had never set foot in New York City, while 'The Shadow Over Innsmouth' suggests that he never visited the New England coast and 'The Dunwich Horror' and 'The Whisperer in Darkness' that he never so much as glanced out a train window at a rural landscape." I suggest the next time the *New York Review* editors call on a distinguished name to write on Lovecraft they make sure that person does his or her homework. ⚅

It Came From the BBC Vaults

Forgotten gems of British horror return from the dead...

A host of filmic horror has been rescued from oblivion in recent years. Among the once-rare titles now on DVD are these fondly remembered BBC teleplays; unseen in America, many were only aired once and never syndicated or released on home video. Archival copies remained in the British Film Institute, only seen by researchers and limited audiences at National Film Theatre retrospectives. Now BFI Video is releasing them to a wider audience. Two are from the '70s, the second golden age of British TV drama. Another is of more recent vintage, but due to the controversy surrounding its original broadcast, was deliberately withheld from public view.

Whistle and I'll Come To You is the oldest, dating from 1968 and not part of the "Ghost Story for Christmas" series that included *A Warning to the Curious* and *The Stone Tape*. It's been controversial amongst those M.R. James fans who've seen it, due to the liberties writer/director Jonathan Miller took with the classic "Oh, Whistle and I'll Come To You, My Lad." James' "young, neat and precise in speech" protagonist is, as embodied by Michael Hordern, middle-aged, neurotic and so incapable of holding a conversation in any but the most academic terms that he's scarcely able to communicate with the staff of the Norfolk hotel where he's on holiday. When something stirs in the empty bed next to his, the sheets moving and stiffening of their own accord, the explanation seems more rooted in psychology (specifically his bachelorhood and probable virginity) than the supernatural. While this approach may frustrate those wanting genuine chills and is not half so clever as Miller imagines, there's no denying the skill of Hordern's performance or the virtues of the moody B&W cinematography.

A Warning to the Curious is more likely to please the Ghosts and Scholars crowd. It's the brainchild of Lawrence Gordon Clark, who brought eight classic ghost stories to British TV, one each Christmas from 1971 to 1978. Five of these were James adaptations; let's hope that *The Stalls of Barchester Cathedral, Lost Hearts, The Ash Tree,* and *The Treasure of Abbott Thomas* are forthcoming.

Whistle's B&W mis-en-scene is replaced by stark color vistas of coastal Norfolk, exquisitely capturing the wintry sunlight. The opening shots, scored to haunting string-and-woodwind, are a shock to those who think all BBC productions of this era drab, studio-bound affairs. Peter Vaughn's diffident amateur archaeologist and treasure hunter, laid off from a clerical job in London and ill at ease amidst the lower classes, is somewhat akin to Hordern's dysfunctional academic, but it's a warmer and more realistic characterization that feels less blatantly imposed on James' story. The period is now the Depression, giving Vaughn's penurious Paxton a less academic stake in finding the lost royal crowns of Anglia.

He bicycles past tottering churches and creaking windmills, over low hills where the red sun limns bare branches and across salt flats where the amber light glitters on brackish pools. In a tumbled churchyard by the sea, he finds a mound said to contain the crowns. It's also covers William Ager, who died of consumption and was the last guardian of the treasure. As he digs, a dark figure stands watching on the distant strand. Later, Paxton will hear a hacking lungless cough in the darkness of his hotel room . . .

That scene gives a real frisson, as does the one in which Paxton desperately attempts to return the cursed treasure. Clark gets far more out of the scenes

WHISTLE AND I'LL
COME TO YOU
1968. B&W, 48 Minutes.
BFI Video Publishing (UK)
PAL all-region DVD. £19.99

A WARNING TO
THE CURIOUS
1972. Color, 50 Minutes. BFI
Video Publishing (UK) PAL
all-region DVD. £15.99

THE STONE TAPE
1972. Color, 75 Minutes. BFI
Video Publishing (UK) PAL
all-region DVD. £19.99

GHOSTWATCH
1992. Color, 90 Minutes. BFI
Video Publishing (UK) PAL
all-region DVD. £19.99

of stalking on a lonely beach than Miller did with similar material and the cast underplays to good effect. My only real cavil (other than with the DVD being devoted to only one less-than-feature-length adaptation rather than a multi-story set) is with the transfer, which is soft and scarcely better than VHS, in sad contrast to the crisp look of *Whistle*.

Nigel Kneale's **The Stone Tape** is the least traditional of all the BBC Christmas ghostlies and the only one without a literary source. Kneale, the most innovative writer in the history of televised fantasy, had been blurring the boundaries between SF and horror since the 50s, when *The Quatermass Experiment* was a media sensation. In *Quatermass and the Pit* (the Hammer film adaptation was released here as *Five Million Years to Earth*), he'd already taken a rationalistic approach to both hauntings and the Lovecraftian theme of Primordial Evil.

Determined to "put the boot to auld Nippon" by finding a new recording medium, a team of researchers from Ryan Electrical Products (whose Scots CEO is never seen, often quoted) are sequestered at Taskerlands, a lonely country estate with a ghostly reputation. All goes smoothly until the team discovers a disused room that was once a US Army store but now contains a flight of stairs leading nowhere, an enigmatic letter to Santa Claus ("all I want for Christmas is please go away"), 30 cans of spam and the parapsychological residue of a 19th century chambermaid, continually screaming as she falls down the stairs. Some members of the team can't hear her wails, but programmer Jill (an overwrought but effective Jane Asher) is able to not just hear but see her. All attempts to record the screams prove futile, but team leader Peter (Michael Bryant), is convinced that solving this mystery is the key to finding the ultimate recording device, a new medium that plays back 3-D images and sound. That "new" medium proves very old; the stones from which the room was built. But when the "stone tape" is accidentally "wiped," the ancient entities whose essence is imprinted "beneath" the first layer of the haunting manifest themselves, with dire consequences for Jill.

In the early '80s I discovered *The Year of the Sex Olympics*, a British paperback collecting three Nigel Kneale teleplays, in the University of North Carolina library. One of the scripts was *The Stone Tape*. Reading it alone in those dusty stacks, I was genuinely creeped out by the climax, in which Jill finds herself on a vast dark plain, hunted amidst towering megaliths by huge grunting shapes with glowing eyes. How, I wondered, did the BBC ever visualize that?

Director Peter Sasdy doesn't, precisely. We only get one menhir, and the giant grunting shadows of Kneale's teleplay (like something out of *The Night Land*) are replaced by reddish blobs and dwarfish cowled forms. Yet the shot-on-video special effects

PARAPSYCHOLOGICAL RESIDUE PLAGUES THE HEROES OF *THE STONE TAPE*.

are more effective and less redolent of old *Doctor Who* than you might think, with Jill's ultimate fate haunting in several senses of the word.

The final BFI release reviewed here is 1992's **Ghostwatch**, which was both Britain's prescient *Blair Witch Project* and belated *War of the Worlds*. A faux-documentary (albeit with glossy BBC production values rather than the now-trendy handheld approach) mimicking the reality show *Crimewatch*, it uses real-life broadcasters to "investigate" poltergeist phenomena at a British council house once inhabited by a notorious pedophile whose corpse was devoured by his starving cats. Popular TV personality Michael Parkinson hosts from the studio, while reporter Sarah Greene and her crew investigate on the scene. It begins low-key and naturalistic, then ratchets up the tension. The finale, in which the studio loses its live feed, then its lights, as the sound of mewling cats drowns out the rest of the audio and _something_ begins to coalesce in the darkness behind Parkinson, is nightmare stuff, not least for its suggestion that the broadcast has become a literal "medium," a massive seance that allows the haunting to manifest not just in the studio but in living rooms across the nation.

One wouldn't expect the BBC to pull off the same Halloween trick fifty-four years after Orson Welles terrified the American listening public, but apparently they succeeded too well. Their phone lines were jammed by angry calls and the press, both respectable and tabloid, reveled in outrage for weeks, particularly after the parents of a teen who allegedly hanged himself after the broadcast told *The Independent* that "I

> Reading the screenplay, I was genuinely creeped out by the climax, in which Jill finds herself on a vast dark plain, hunted amidst towering megaliths by huge grunting shapes with glowing eyes.

blame the BBC — it's all their fault." Chagrined, the BBC promised never to broadcast the program again, and all earlier attempts at securing a home video release were rebuffed.

But is it still scary if you're in on the joke? Yes. As Kim Newman argues in his liner notes, it's doubtful that writer Stephen Volk and director Ruth Manning meant to fool anyone; the mockumentary format is "no more than the television version of the first chapter of *Turn of the Screw*" or the more elaborate lengths that James Hogg underwent in 1824 to "convince" readers that *Confessions of a Justified Sinner* had been recovered from a peat bog. In other words, part of the fine old "told for the truth" tradition.

All of these disks have sparse but well-chosen extras, including Kim Newman and Nigel Kneale's commentary on *The Stone Tape*, Ramsey Campbell's reading of "Oh, Whistle, and I'll Come to You, My Lad" and Volk and Manning's articulate commentary on *Ghostwatch*. They are available for £14.99-£19.99 directly from the BFI at www.bfi.org.uk/videocat, from www.amazon.co.uk, and from www.blackstar.co.uk. While all are region-free, you'll need either a DVD player that converts from PAL (most all-region players do , of course) or a PC with DVD drive. 𝄐

A typical "Monster Boomer," Ian McDowell grew up reading Famous Monsters of Filmland *and* Castle of Frankenstein. *As a teenager, he performed in community theatre with future make-up effects genius Tom Savini, whose ape suit he borrowed on several memorable occasions.*

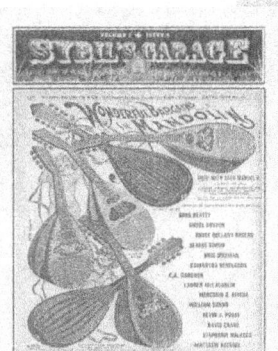

film comment ✳ by Carole Buggé

People Eat Seafood Eat People

Why **The Host** is such an exceptional movie.

When we first see the title character in Bong Joon-Ho's remarkable film *The Host*, it is hanging upside down underneath a bridge over the Han River, like an enormous sleeping bat. In fact, the bewildered onlookers aren't even sure if it's alive — they actually suspect at first that it's some kind of inanimate object. (We know better, of course — we have seen the incident leading up to the creation of this mutant miscreant.)

Their misguided impression is abruptly punctured when the creature propels itself off the bridge and plunges into the swirling grey waters of the Han River. Turns out, not only is it alive, but it has an agenda — one that, predictably, involves eating (and regurgitating) human beings.

But that is the only predictable thing about this original and inventive movie from the Republic of Korea. *The Host* manages to tread the fine line between expectation and cliché, always staying one step ahead of the viewer, both teasing and inverting monster movie

clichés in ways that both honor and transcend the genre.

The mutant beast that terrorizes the residents of Seoul is a malevolent, clever creature — as indifferent to human suffering as any mythological white whale. With the help of its prehensile tail, it can swing from girder to girder more efficiently than Tarzan. Once on land, it clumps along rapidly on its two stocky legs to thumping percussion background music so insistent that one imagines every past and present cast member of *Stomp!* was recruited during the recording of the soundtrack.

But the chief evil in Korea, the film slyly suggests, springs from the bloated, incompetent governmental bureaucracy — and, it is implied, its American influence. Every time an American character makes an appearance in the movie, you can bet they are up to no good. (In a wonderful reversal of racial stereotyping, at one point the Korean protagonist is confronted by a clueless, cross-eyed American scientist).

The first and most malevolent American we meet is the head scientist at an army base morgue (Scott Wilson), who orders his Korean assistant to dump an obscene amount of formaldehyde into the sink. His justification for what turns out to be an act of eco-terrorism? The bottles are dusty, and he abhors dust "more than anything." (The premise is actually based on a real-life incident: in 2000, Albert McFarland, an American civilian mortician at the Yongsan military base, did in fact instruct his staff to discard 120 litres of formaldehyde. The chemicals eventually found their way into the Han, source of Seoul's drinking water, and set off anti-American protests in South Korea.)

This opening exposition is dispensed with cleanly and quickly: one brief fast forward shows there is something growing in the water, then we jump six years later, to 2006, when the residents of Seoul see the creature hanging from a bridge over the river.

The protagonists of *The Host* are the Parks — an ordinary enough Korean version of a dysfunctional family, except for a daughter who is a champion archer. However, as it digs deeper into the heart of darkness (not only of the monster, but of the paranoid and incompetent government bureaucracy), the film becomes a meditation on the nature of loyalty, courage and tenacity — and, perhaps most tellingly, family.

Though the entire Park family collectively fills the role of hero, the central (and most compromised) protagonist is Gung Don, who lives with his elderly father and adolescent daughter in a corrugated tin shack along the side of the Han River, serving snacks to the picnickers who line the banks of the muddy, fast running river. When we first see him, he is dozing among the shelves of instant noodles and dried squid — when his father wakens him and sends him off to serve a picnicking family, he absent-mindedly bites one of the tentacles off of the squid he is to bring them. At this sight, the film viewer squirms uncomfortably, knowing that this is probably the last time a human will be eating a sea creature, and that the tables will soon be turned.

And we are right: All hell is about to break loose. In a scene that is like a horrifying parody of evolution, the monster emerges from the waves of the grey, roiling river. This creature has come to walk (or run) on land, all right, but its appetite is even more primeval and terrifying than the raptors in *Jurassic Park*. Before the viewer has a chance to get a good look at the clomping, flesh-stomping monster, it has destroyed more picnickers than a swarm of killer bees, and snatched away Gung Don's daughter, Hyun-seo.

As in *Little Miss Sunshine,* to which *The Host* has often been compared, the characters in this film band together to save the beloved youngest member of the family — not from dragon-lady mothers in this case — but from a real dragon. Each member of the family has a scene of heroism and sacrifice; the performances of Kang-ho Song as the hapless Gung Don and Ah-sung Ko as the courageous and resourceful Hyun-seo are especially strong. Though the climax feels painfully delayed at times, the filmmaker's use of the older sister's archery skill to defeat the monster is no less than brilliant.

This is one of the wettest films in recent memory, and the deluge of rain evokes (perhaps purposefully) Kurosawa's masterpiece *The Seven Samurai*. Water imagery is everywhere — from the first scene on, with the dumping of toxic formaldehyde into the city's drainage system. Rain pelts the characters throughout the film, and liquids leak constantly from sewers, bodies, disinfectant spray canisters — even beer cans spring holes and spurt their contents into the grey atmosphere hanging over Seoul. Even the parting shot is wet — a soft snow falls over the tin shack which still sits along the banks of the river.

That *The Host* is allegorical is beyond question — but an allegory for what? Perhaps Bong Joon-Ho's social critique is purposefully broad. The government is worse than useless; science and the military are impotent against this mutated monster from the polluted Han River. But it seems no coincidence that Gung Don's hair, which is dyed blond at the beginning of the movie, eventually reverts to its natural black color as he gradually transforms from a screw-up to a truly heroic action hero — perhaps another subtle commentary on the insidious incompetence of the Western influence. And the governmental obsession with a deadly virus believed to be carried by the monster seems to be a clear reference to the obsessive Western paranoia about Communism.

Bong Joon-Ho, (who co-authored the screenplay along with Ha Jun-weon and Baek Cheol-hyeon) has a Shakespearean ability to create comic relief in moments of high tension — his willingness to take a risk and flip the tone of a single scene within seconds is exhilarating. A touching mourning sequence near the beginning of the film slides skillfully into slapstick, and before we realize it, we are laughing helplessly at the excessive grief of the bereaved family, and giggling at the pomposity of a stumbling government official. The risks pays off — when an audience really doesn't know what's coming next, they are putty in a director's hand. Bong Joon-Ho has us, and he's not about to let go.

Lee Byeong-woo's score ranges from the heart-pounding rhythms of the monster's forays onto land to more romantic, sweeping melodies, effectively combining a traditionally classical Western sound with a more chordal Eastern sensibility.

The film itself is a Korean-Japanese co-production, and the special effects are the result of a collaboration between New Zealand's Weta Digital and San Francisco's The Orphanage, making *The Host* a truly international enterprise. At a time when Kim Jong-Il's shenanigans in nearby North Korea are giving our government the willies, Bong Joon-Ho has created a monster that knows how to make us squirm in a way that is as unexpected as it is terrifying. ᘓ

Laurell K. Hamilton

BUILDING THE VAMPIRE HUNTER'S WORLD

interview by

Michael McCarty &
Cristopher Hennessey-DeRose

She's become the most popular author of
monsterotic literature in a decade.
How does Anita Blake's creator feel
about all her undead literary offspring?

Since we're talking with you, Laurell, from a
magazine named after H.P. Lovecraft, what
are your thoughts on his work? The myths
he created are still alive and disturbing seven
decades after his death. Lovecraft anthologies full of fresh stories from new writers come out
almost every year. Most writers of the macabre will
site him as one of their early influences, me included. The fact that this magazine exists is proof that
Lovecraft's genius continues to influence us all
today and for generations to come.

Who are some of your favorite vampire writers and books? "Camilla" by Sheridan Le Fanu is still a sensuous and frightening tale, even after a century. The writing is smoother and more "modern" than a lot of stories from the same time period. The nonfiction book that stands out for me is *The Natural History Of The Vampire* by Anthony Masters. I first discovered it in high school, and it is still one of my favorite reference books for vamps. It was one of the earliest books I came across that had a large bibliography in the back. One of the things I've learned in reference books is that if the book does not contain an extensive list of books that that book, itself, has referenced, then you are often getting merely the opinion of one person, the author of that book. I also have a copy of *The Vampire Book* by J. Gordon Melton on my shelves. It contains more popular culture and covers more modern cases, and also has a nice bibliography. And no list is complete without Anne Rice's *Interview With The Vampire*. That was, and still is, a most lovely book.

Was getting pigeonholed as a "vampire writer" ever a concern to you early on in your career? No. First, I don't think of myself as a vampire writer. Because there are lots of other kinds of monsters in my books. Funny, how no one ever says someone is a "werewolf writer." My main character isn't even a vampire. But there is something about putting a vamp in your stories that does indeed make people label you as a vampire writer. My books are mysteries, romance, fantasy — some people have even called them science fiction — but because there are some horror elements in every book, and vampires in most, I did get pigeonholed. But I'm okay with that. A pigeonhole is only a burden if you don't like where you've been shelved. I am writing exactly what I want to write in exactly the way I want to write it. There is nothing better as a writer than that.

Do you allow your characters the luxury of taking the story in an unexpected turn, or do you stick to the original outline? Any examples? Outlines were meant to bend, or break — at least for me. I will never sacrifice characterization for plot. The plot can be reworked; character growth, once screwed up, is almost irretrievable. I don't always like the choices my characters make, but I am amazed that they were "alive" enough to make the choice, to argue with me. I've finally made peace with the fact that I'm wrong a lot.

Example: Early in the series I would have bet good money that Jean-Claude would never be a romantic lead. I was so tired of the vampire as a romantic figure. I mean they are walking corpses, what's so hot about that? That was honestly how Anita and I both felt in the first book, *Guilty Pleasures*. I swore that I'd kill him before he ever became a true romantic lead. It would take me two more books before I began to understand that I couldn't kill Jean-Claude off, that losing him would hurt Anita — and me. Anita is like most of my friends: I can give them dating advice, but they rarely take it. Career advice, I don't even try. I would like to see Anita truly happy for more than moments at a time, but I no longer know the route we will be taking to get there.

If they were real, what nightclub would you go to: The Laughing Corpse, Narcissus In Chains, Guilty Pleasures or another one in the Anita Blake world? Danse Macabre if I was going out for an evening with just my husband. Burnt Offerings, if I was doing a family night out.

What are the origins of the Church of Eternal Life? How important is it to the Anita Blake series? When I sit down to write, I always think, *if this true, then what?* It's part of how you're told to write science fiction, but I think it is equally valid with horror or fantasy. If vampires are real in Anita's world, and if they have rights and freedoms, the whole nine yards, then what next? What would that mean for a modern-day America? The Church of Eternal Life was one of the things that came from that early brainstorming session: the idea that if vamps were real, that people would want to be one. Here was a church that didn't require a leap of faith. You want to know what's it like to be dead, as a church member. Most people don't believe in the immortal soul anymore, not really. I think if you don't sweat that little detail, then people would be signing up in droves for a little guaranteed immortality. It's still one of the most disturbing ideas that I've come up with, at least to me.

I'm giving you an open mic — let's talk about your work. What do you have to say about your following books:

Guilty Pleasures: Welcome to the world of Anita Blake – zombie raiser and vampire hunter. A world not dissimilar to our own, if we woke up tomorrow and everything that went bump in the night was real.

I intended for this to be a mystery series with horror overtones, combining hard-boiled detective mysteries with horror. This is also where we first meet Jean-Claude, who was to play a larger part than I ever intended, and Edward the hitman, who kills monsters because humans are too easy. Edward was intended to be so alien to everyone's experiences that he would truly be someone no one could really like — respect maybe, but not like.

Laughing Corpse: With this book we further explore Anita's world and what her life is like. We get to see where Anita draws lines. Who's the bigger monster? Humans willing to do anything for money, or monsters themselves? What did it mean to be a monster? Not all monsters are easily recognizable just by looking.

Circus Of The Damned: What does it mean to have power over another — and how do you handle it when the other is you? It was while writing this book that I realized I couldn't follow my plan to kill Jean-Claude. I introduced the character of Richard to forestall Jean-Claude's ever becoming a romantic lead. I swore long and loud to everyone who would listen that Anita and Jean-Claude would never be a couple. Edward makes another return, and we introduce Larry Kirkland, zombie raiser in training.

The Lunatic Café: This was actually one of my very few trunk books I have that got cannibalized and became *The Lunatic Café*. It was also where we learned a lot more about the werewolves and their culture. I drew heavily on Greek and Norse mythologies for the hierarchy and language the wolves would use amongst themselves. Edward is back yet again — a character I truly thought everyone would find despicable in some sense. But he had already developed quite a following of his own.

Bloody Bones: This was Anita's first out-of-town adventure. Branson, Missouri's answer to Nashville. We also see our first fey in this series. I thought I knew a lot about the fey when I wrote this book. Later, when I started research for the Merry Gentry series, I realized how little I really knew about Celtic myth and folklore.

The Killing Dance: I originally wanted to title this book *Dance Macabre* after Jean-Claude's dance club. But my publisher didn't want me to use the same title as the Stephen King book, so it got retitled after a sexual euphemism amongst the werewolves. Which is only fair, as they are one of the focuses of this story. This is also the first time we have actual sex on paper.

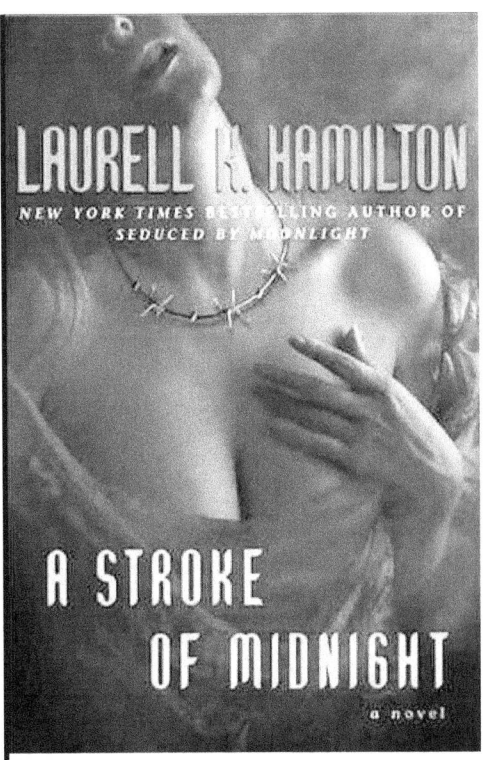

> *"In researching for Anita, I talked to combat veterans, and was privileged to have them share their experiences with me. Because Anita has a violence level that is far above most police work."*

Burnt Offerings: This story focused more on the vampires and their hierarchy. What was their culture like? How did they run their own group? So we got to see the politics that are inherent in the vampire life via the Council, who are basically the vampire government. We also learn more about the wereleopards than Anita ever wanted to know.

Blue Moon: Out of town again for Anita this time in Tennessee. We find out that not every werewolf pack works the same, though the vampires are frighteningly deadly everywhere we go. We also continue our learning curve on the wereleopards. Sex again!

Obsidian Butterfly: Anita goes to Edward's aid in New Mexico. This one is the Edward book. I was just as curious as fans were as to who Edward was really. What was his day-to-day life like? Surely he had one. Where did he live? What did he do when he wasn't killing things?

This was also the hardest monster to come up with. What would frighten someone like Edward? It took me weeks of research to find the monster that'd scare Edward — and anything that would scare Edward certainly scared the heck out of me.

Narcissus In Chains: I honestly set out to simplify Anita's love life in this book. Boy, was I wrong. More and more complex it grows.

Cerulean Sin: This book is where Anita faces the realities of what her life is. What she had planned for herself is never going to come around. What is love? What is lust? What is friendship? How do you tell them apart? Is violence always the answer? Is there a different way to accomplish your goals without killing or being killed?

Kiss Of Shadows: This was the debut of Merry Gentry, fairy princess/private eye. Like Anita, this is set in our world with a twist. The fey have taken up residence in the United States when they were thrown out of Europe.

I wrote five Anita books in a row and really needed a break. Besides, no one was writing the fey the way I wanted to see them.

Caress Of Twilight: This book is about power. Power of love. Power of politics. Merry is beginning to realize what it means to rule. To truly rule not for yourself but for those you're ultimately responsible for. She is starting to see what that means, and what it may cost her in the long run.

Anita Blake has come to understand the world is not simply black and white, but has shades of gray in it as well, and it's happened in a very natural progression. Was this something planned from the start, or did it happen as the characters matured? When I first researched Anita's world, I talked to policemen in depth about their job. I learned something of the cost of the job. I watched my brother-in-law go from bright and shiny to tired. As I continued to research for Anita, I talked to combat veterans, and was privileged to have them share some of their experiences with me. Because Anita really has a violence level that is far above most police work. I use to joke she lived in a combat zone until I did one book where she visited what amounted to a real combat zone, and she was out of her depth. In book nine, *Obsidian Butterfly*, we visited Edward's world, and saw something closer to real soldiering.

It was frightening. But as I talked to men, and some women, about their lives, I realized that to keep Anita at the level of violence where she was would have a price. Part of that price is innocence, and the knowledge that the world is not black and white, and answers are not as simple as they seem.

Anita had to go through this process, or it would have felt like a betrayal of those people who spoke with me and shared their experiences.

Is networking at conventions and other places writers gather essential to long-term success these days? Yes, and no. At the beginning of your career: Very yes. First, dress for success. You can be dramatic, by all means be yourself, but don't show up in jeans and a T-shirt, unless you look *really* good in jeans and a T-shirt. Be clean, neat, presentable. This is a business — treat it that way. I highly recommend dressing nice, so you don't look hungry.

By that, I mean: If you look and act like you need this job, need this contract, need to sell a book, people will run from you, or treat you badly. If you act businesslike — and not like the fate of the world, or your sanity, rides on some editor's opinion — you'll do better. Trust me. I speak from experience. Act confident, no matter how you feel inside. Have business cards made, but sure they look good, not cheap. You can do some pretty nice ones on most computer printers these days. But they must not look cheap.

You can be the best writer in the world, but at a convention no one is reading your writing, they're just seeing you. Remember that. If you present yourself badly, you hurt yourself. You don't have to be brilliant, just professional. I had breakfast meetings, lunch meetings, dinner meetings, snack meeting, every kind of meetings, over the years. I think through all those meetings, I sold one short story, and no books. Was it wasted time? No. Some fellow members of my writing group — Deborah Millitello and Mark Sumner, to name two — sold more short stories than I did at the same meetings. It led to a book contract for Mark. So it wasn't

wasted. You never know what contact will pay off. I met my first agent at a convention, though that is highly unusual.

But be wary: Some people who go to conventions are not always as good as they seem. Anyone can claim to be editing an anthology or to be an agent. Get the agent's client list. Find out who they represent. If they are legitimate, then they will have people you can call, who will tell you what kind of job they're doing as agent. Though bear in mind that the agent isn't going to give you names of people who think they suck.

Your grandmother told you horror tales taken from the hills of Arkansas, leaving you with the thought, "Rawhide and bloody bones will get you if you aren't good." Do you ever think back to those stories for influence or inspiration? I don't really think back to my grandmother's stories for inspiration, but I think that I have absorbed those stories into the pores of my being.

It was simply an accepted fact that ghosts were real, that the dead didn't always rest easy, that things could move by themselves, and that simple things could be frightening. I used to blame my family's penchant for macabre true stories, and other real-life tragedies, for my dark turn of mind. Recently, I've had to rethink that. My daughter is eight, and she loves mummies. Her favorite book for ages was *Cinderella Skelton,* where all the characters are ghouls and such, and the main character loses a lot more than just her slipper running down the stairs. It's made me remember that long before my mother's death, when I played cowboys and cowgirls, it wasn't enough for the chairs to be tall cliffs. No, we had to have a pit of rattlesnakes at the bottom of the cliff, so we'd be bitten to death. A fall just wasn't horrible enough. My daughter's childhood is making me rethink my own. Apparently, it wasn't early tragedies that made me this way — maybe, just maybe, it was the way I came.

Anything else you'd like to add? If anyone would like more info on Anita or Merry, we have the first chapters of each up on our website: www.laurellkhamilton.org. We also have a message board, images of the various book covers from all over the world, links to nifty sites, photos from various cons and signings, more interviews, all kinds of Anita and Merry merchandise, and a link to Pet Finders and Granite City, Illinois, APA in case you're looking for a new friend who really needs a home.

And lastly, please remember to spay or neuter your pet. It is the kind thing to do. *Ᏽ*

Urban Nightmares

HORROR IN AN AGE OF TERROR

by Larry Tritten

Ever since 2001 — September 11, to be precise — the phrase "urban horror" has acquired dramatic new overtones of meaning. I don't remember when it first started to appear as a phrase designed to peg a subgenre of contemporary horror fiction. I think it postdates the early work of Stephen King. In any case, it seems essentially gratuitous. Does it undertake to draw a distinction between horror fiction that takes place in a setting where one can catch a cab and one where the bovine and equine population rivals that of the people? And is *The Stepford Wives* suburban horror fiction? Then what would be an example of exurban horror fiction?

Ironically, I think the label was invented by writers and editors who specialize in the stuff, notwithstanding the fact that genre labels are bad for writers. Call Harlan Ellison a science- fiction writer to his face and you will quickly (and probably by way of object lesson) find out why. The aforementioned labels appeal to a fan mentality, but they are a form of typecasting that tend to put a writer's work in a commercial ghetto. To draw an analogy, Sean Connery's career probably would have ended with James Bond if he had been known as an espionage actor. When Poe wrote "The Tell-Tale Heart" there was no such thing as horror fiction, and when Jules Verne wrote *From the Earth to the Moon* there was no such thing as science fiction. There was simply fiction, which of course was of widely varying types.

As for urban horror fiction, it has clearly been spectacularly upstaged by reality. Were you more effectively horrified by the TV news shows and newspapers of September 2001 or by *Rosemary's Baby* and *The Exorcist*? But, in fact, the horror provided by the real world has always been more spectacular than that in fiction. Last summer, approaching Dresden in a Lufthansa airliner, I experienced a feeling something like a cross between Weltschmerz and Sartrean-style nausea, thinking about those days in February, 1945, when hundreds of other airplanes approached the city, which they would subsequently leave in an inferno of flame along with the corpses of something like 100,000 men, women, and children. That was, to be sure, quintessential urban horror and with no supernatural element whatever. And it was just one such scenario among scores of others, e.g., Hiroshima, Nagasaki, Coventry, Berlin, London, etc.

While the bombs were falling on those cities and hundreds of thousands of people were being exterminated, the horror movies of the day featured werewolves, vampires, and ghosts. Does it seem ironic that in such a world an anthropomorphic wolf would be expected to give one bad dreams?

In retrospect, the horror movies of the thirties and forties seem almost as quaint as fairy tales. The monsters were mythical rather than the serial killers of the real world that would come to dominate the genre beginning with *Blood Feast* and *Two Thousand Maniacs* in the 1950s — monsters that owed their dark inspiration to real people like Jack the Ripper, Ed Gein, Ted Bundy, etc. My personal preference is for the classic horror movies and stories, although the evil they portray is in the purest sense less frightening because its archetypal monsters and ghosts are fundamentally implausible (except to a hardcore occultist or Christian).

The sense of horror aroused by a maniac wielding an ax is almost indisputably greater than that provoked by a Hungarian count with a thick accent, wings, and sharp incisors. If scaring you is the sole raison d'etre of a horror story, then lycanthropes and ambulatory corpses have tough competition with real-world psychopaths. Anyway, there is something dispiriting to me about the popularity of the latter with contemporary movie audiences. As the protagonist of one of my (urban horror) stories observes:

"When I was a kid the monsters in horror movies were vampires, werewolves, and the like, and in the final scene the stake was driven or the silver bullet was fired, evil was conquered, and we felt good about it. But today's horror movies are about serial killers and other such types of human monsters who for the most part do their work with blades, and at the end of the movie Jason or Freddy is still there, invulnerable, ready for the next go around, evil prospers, and the subliminal perk for the movie watcher is to experience a sustained vicarious sense of terror and lousy feeling." Which is to say it's an exercise in masochism.

We are, to be sure, perverse beasts, animals for whom evil can have an intellectual rationale. Consider Hannibal Lecter. Or Leopold and Loeb. Or Adolf Hitler. Or Osama bin Laden. All but one of whom are real people. Small wonder that the city, modern man's habitat, is the perfect setting for horror stories. Urban horror is a first cousin of film noir, whose world is one of the night-time city — back alleys and shadowy office buildings, crowded night clubs and neon-lit (in black and white!) streets. There is a tacit implication that the rustic world is by comparison idyllic. There are those

> Horror fiction has clearly been spectacularly upstaged by reality. Were you more horrified by the TV news of September 2001, or by *The Exorcist?*

romantics like Rousseau who make a case for the innocence and contentment of primitive man in "a state of nature," or Edward Hicks whose painting "The Peaceable Kingdom" depicts a world in which animals, both predators and prey, live together in harmony. But of course the reality is that nature is, in the words of Tennyson, "red in tooth and claw." The tranquil beauty of nature is in all instances an illusion. In nature all creatures from parasites to primates are fated to regard each other as comestibles, the natural order being in essence a horror story incarnate.

Whether the setting is metropolitan or bucolic, the writer or film maker has a broad choice in the matter of the technique used to exacerbate our emotions. The "splatterpunk" writers and directors of the aforementioned slasher movies use graphic imagery, exhibiting relentlessly vivid renderings (!) of people being murdered and mutilated, and in these movies the victims are invariably beautiful young women, which adds a perversely psychosexual element to the act. In contrast, there are those who choose to evoke horror by way of establishing a gradual mood rather than using images calculated to shock. An analogy can be drawn between the two approaches and the familiar debate about which is more sexually exciting — flagrant nudity or dishabille, the argument for the latter being that it gives importance to the value of mystery, allowing one's imagination to play a lively part in the process of stimulation. One can extend the analogy by comparing shock imagery and the development of mood with rape and seduction.

In the movies these opposites are represented by, say, *The Texas Chainsaw Massacre* (whose title alone is an assault on our nervous system) and a movie like *Poltergeist*. Only after seeing *Poltergeist* two or three times did it occur to me that there is not a single death in the movie. It manages to be a kinetic horror movie without recourse to any homicide. The realization should be enough to make the most avid splatterpunk willing to trade in their cutlery for a jar of ectoplasm.

There are horror fiction writers whose work is so nasty that it effectively rapes the imagination. I won't presume to say that this is an absolutely improper approach. Writers make up their own minds about such matters and the only really reprehensible thing is to write badly, to deliver the shocks in prose that scarcely exceeds semi-literacy. Yet art should be allowed libertine (check the word's etymology) indulgences, and it is important that the imagination not be policed by censors.

In any case, I'll cite three of my favorite horror stories in the interest of making the case for how a good writer can terrify a reader without

>> continued on page 60

ILLUSTRATION BY BENOIT

WHEN SHE GREW UP,
SHE WOULD MAKE THEM LISTEN —
ONCE AND FOR ALL.

Sometimes You Have To Shout About It

by Darrell Schweitzer

When Caroline was born (so she was told later), she came out of the womb screaming, and the doctor allegedly remarked, "Good strong lungs. Maybe she'll be an opera singer when she grows up." But by the time she was old enough to run around the neighborhood and blast people's eardrums to near deafness (or at least to the point of angrily slammed windows and doors) it was clear that she might have the volume, but there was no particular beauty in her voice.

"Christ, that kid is loud," people said, and what very few friends she had in the early grades asked her, "Why do you make so much noise?"

That wasn't to be the last time anyone asked her that, though her mother, by and large, gave up on the point, and when her father took her to the zoo or to the park or celebrated her birthday or otherwise paid attention to her (however infrequently) and managed to keep her quiet, he never ruined the affair by asking such questions.

But most of the time her father was "away" and her mother was preoccupied with something she said Caroline was too young to understand.

Father went away for good when Caroline was nine. One night she got up late because she had a sore throat, or she had a bad dream, or both (details became confused as she was later forced to tell this story over and over) and for all she knew that it was really unlikely that she would get much comfort from either parent, she came downstairs, and knocked gently on the door to her father's study (which was always locked, even when he was in it).

But she paused when she heard Father and Mother arguing in there, in tones that sounded as much fearful as angry.

Certainly no one heard her, and she stood alone in the darkened hall as the noise got worse and things crashed and there were awful, burning smells, then the impossible sound of a roaring wind, as loud as an express train. The whole house shook with it and something thumped hard, once, twice, three times against the door until it seemed about to burst off its hinges.

Then there was silence, and blood flowed like a wave under the door, eclipsing the light from within, splashing over Caroline's slippers until her feet were soaked and the cuffs of her pajamas were glued to her ankles.

That was when Caroline started screaming. She ran out into the chilly November night, screaming, until windows came up and people shouted, "Shut up you crazy brat!"

She was still screaming when the police found her, hours later, minus her slippers and covered with mud, huddled among some trees in the park, almost hoarse now, so that the noise she made was more of a wheezing moan than a scream, and she tasted blood in her mouth.

After that she was wrapped up in warm blankets and treated kindly by lots of people who made stupid noises at her and talked in near baby-talk in a pathetic attempt to "get down to her level," as someone (even Caroline, years later) might have put it. She was made to tell her story again and again, but still she screamed a lot, and therapists, in a hospital, gave her drugs to make her sleep, and told her when she woke up that everything had been a bad dream.

But no one believed her story. Her father was gone, yes, but there was no trace of blood, and nothing was broken in the house, and her mother, on visits, refused to explain further. She overheard the doctors and her mom and someone who might have been a lawyer talking about "desertion" once, but when everybody realized Caroline was listening, they shut the door to her room and went down the hall to the lounge.

What really must have been a dream, Caroline concluded, was the time her mother slipped into her room after visiting hours and sat down beside her bed in the dark. Mother was crying, which was amazing, and she whispered, "Honey, I want you to know that whatever happens, I still love you."

Then Caroline turned and buried her face in her pillow and screamed as hard as she could, but no one heard her, and Mother was gone.

That was the greatest discovery in her life so far, that if she screamed into her pillow and no one heard her, she could pretend she was getting better and would be allowed to go home, and she could keep her secret from her mother, from the therapists, from everyone.

Her secret, which indeed she had kept, even through the relentless interrogations, was the real reason she made so much noise in the first place, why she screamed — into her pillow now, unheard by everyone else, which was actually much better.

It was because if she screamed loudly enough, it was like punching through a barrier into another world, and sounds came back to her, not echoes, but answers. She was conversing with something or someone very far away, and she had to shout to make herself heard. Many nights she would scream into her pil-

low for a while, then lie awake for hours, listening to the darkness make its reply, comforting her and soothing her, telling strange stories and promising the answers to things she didn't understand.

If no one else listened to her, if no one else believed her, there was always this other, this answerer, who did.

Once she even asked the darkness, "What am I going to be when I grow up?" and a voice like a winter wind rattling dead leaves replied, "Anything you want. Anything at all."

II

That must have been a dream about her mother saying she loved her, because when Caroline came back home, Mom had a new boyfriend, whose name was Jack. He pretended to be her uncle, but wasn't. He didn't like Caroline at all. Mom would not let "Uncle" Jack hurt her, and once she even grabbed his wrist when he raised a coke bottle to smack her, but otherwise Mom did everything Jack told her to do, as if she were his slave. The two of them were away a lot, or when they were home they were locked in the basement (which had been converted into a laboratory of some sort; Caroline was never allowed down there), and sometimes there were the awful smells and noises.

In summer, Caroline took to sleeping on the porch, or in the hammock in the back yard. This was encouraged. She wasn't wanted in the house.

She always brought a pillow to scream into.

She pretty much raised herself. When she was twelve, she decided she wanted to be a dancer when she grew up, and in the times when Mom and Jack were somewhere else, she would spend long hours curled up in front of the TV watching videotapes of Fred Astaire and Ginger Rogers movies, sometimes with the sound off, just watching the two graceful black and white figures whirling across the screen, while the darkness whispered to her in the voice she had known all her life.

Meanwhile, Jack started to bring strangers into the house, a lot of them, late at night. Sometimes they didn't seem to arrive. They were merely there. They spoke with foreign accents or even in foreign languages, or chanted, or sang behind closed doors, and the smells were worse then. Caroline could tell that her mother didn't like this. Mom looked hollow-eyed and even afraid, exhausted all the time, but she still wouldn't say anything to Caroline, who knew that when this sort of stuff was happening, it was time to make herself scarce.

She spent hours in the local library, doing her homework, reading books about far places, or drawing leaping, flying, costumed figures in her notebooks. She had given up on the idea of being a dancer by the time she was thirteen, because she knew she'd never get lessons and it was probably already too late to begin, anyway. She'd fallen in love with comic books and sometimes pretended she was a superhero with a secret identity. Not heroine. It never occurred to her that comic-book characters really had gender, or anything under those tights.

More seriously, she thought she'd like to draw *X-Men* when she grew up, even if, right now, her figures tended to be lumpy and misshapen. She knew she'd have to study hard.

But it was hard enough just to get by in school. She was out of the house so much that it was a struggle to keep up appearances. Not that she cared much about appearances the way the popular girls did, not that she bothered with makeup or painting her nails, but she did like to be clean like anybody else, and have fresh underwear. Yet if she spent all night at the library, or at the train station reading under the lights while pretending to be waiting for a late train, and then came home to find the house full of strange people and noises and odd flickering lights and had to sleep out in the yard, it showed. She hated going to school with the knees of her pants dirty or leaf bits in her hair. By the time she was in junior high, she figured out how to slip into the girl's locker room at six o'clock in the morning and use the shower – until she got caught at it one day.

"My mom hasn't been paying the water bills," she said, but she didn't think she was believed.

"Caroline," the school counselor said, in a voice so drippingly sympathetic that it was all Caroline could do not to laugh in her face, "is everything all right at home?"

"Yeah," she said. "Everything's fine."

That was the funny part, as she laughed and cried and screamed into her pillow – or sometimes, when she was alone in the park, into the sky and she didn't give a damn who heard her – because things were not fine.

It was, again, almost November. She was sleeping out in the yard more often than not because she was afraid to go into the house, and she was likely to get frostbite in that damn hammock, even if she did wear a heavy coat and sleep under the same old muddy blanket as always.

She lay there in the dark. Her face was cold. Her teeth chattered. She was angry. By now she was fourteen and had torn up her notebooks in a fit of rage, and wasn't going to be an artist any more when she grew up. No, she was going to become a scientist and learn a way to blow up the world and do it. No one cared about her. No one believed anything she said, and so, she decided, it didn't matter what she said – because she was always a mess, because she was crazy and everyone knew it and she lived in a house with a yard that was overgrown with weeds and looked condemned or haunted or both. So it didn't matter that time when one of the goth kids at school sidled up to her in the hallway and said, "Caroline, are you a witch? Wanna join our coven?"

"Yes," she said, "I am a witch. I've sold my soul to the Devil!"

She said it with such conviction that the goth-kid seemed to just melt. He ran away, and Caroline laughed so hard and so long and so loudly that it made a scene, and everybody was staring, and she didn't give a damn if they did.

But most of them didn't call her a witch. Somebody saw her scrounging for pizza out of a dumpster and the next day it was all over school and kids greeted her with, "Eew, gross . . ." and said among themselves, but making sure she could hear them, "Caroline's going to be a bag-lady when she grows up. Maybe she's one already."

"Yeah, everything's fine," she told the counselor again and again.

So she lay in the hammock in the late October dark on a night when she was certain that Jack and dear old Mom, who supposedly loved her no matter what, had murdered someone. She saw them dragging a girl not much older than herself, somebody she didn't know, who didn't seem to be wearing much clothing,

down into the basement. She had even been able to sneak a glimpse of what was going on down there, just this once. The struggling girl must have made Mom and Uncle Jack careless.

The curtains were open, so Caroline, crouching on the back porch, could peer in through the back door and see down the basement steps. A crowd of people waited at the base of the stairs, their faces horribly pale, all of them dressed in black, their outstretched hands like claws – and then the basement door slammed shut and she knew, as she so often did, that it was time to make herself invisible.

That night, after she'd screamed into her crumpled blanket for a long time and finally punched a hole through the darkness into that other place where the answers came from, the darkness began to speak to her, its voice more distinct than she had ever heard it before. The darkness touched her. Its touch was hard and warm, but somehow comforting, as if strong, invisible hands caressed her. That night she looked up from out of her hammock and saw that the whole house was ablaze with light. She watched as all of the windows of the house slid open simultaneously, silently. In complete silence her mother and Uncle Jack, now dressed in black robes, leaned out of the upstairs bedroom and floated into the air, ascending like smoke, while from all the other windows, even the barred ones in the basement window-wells, other people rose up, dozens of them, like a cloud of enormous bats, their black robes fluttering like wings as they spiraled up, up, blotting out the moon.

Meanwhile the darkness whispered in her ear, and something with hard, warm hands touched her and comforted her.

That night was Halloween, not that any trick-or-treaters ever came to Caroline's house, or anyone came at this hour, as it was well past midnight, but she knew that on this night (and also in the spring, at the end of April) Mom and Jack and the rest had their big "do's" and this must have been one of them, for which occasion they had murdered that girl, whoever she was.

The thing in the darkness took her by the hand, and helped her out of the hammock, then led her into a dance as the bat-things scattered from the face of the Moon. Pale light rippled over the back yard and she began to see what she was dancing with, a male figure, naked, utterly black, like a computer graphic, she thought, something that could morph into any shape; but now it was this gleaming, handsome man, and she danced with him as if she were Ginger Rogers and he was Fred Astaire; and they whirled around and around with the music turned off, listening to the darkness, which spoke to her from very far away and told her that she was safe and everything would be fine and she could be anything, anything at all that she wanted to be when she grew up.

"Yeah, I'm a witch all right, just like my mom," she said aloud, as if concluding that conversation with the goth-boy at school. "I'm pretty sure."

But all that might have been a dream. She knew she would have to wait until dawn, when Mom and Jack and the rest would return from their distant sabbat. Then the friend she had called out of the darkness would confront them, and command them, and begin to feed.

Then she would be sure.

She shouted. She didn't care who heard. ⋒

ILLUSTRATION BY MAUREEN DAINTY

AS PLAGUES GO,
THIS ONE WAS JUST
DOWNRIGHT BIBLICAL.

Crickets, Everywhere

by Ken Rand

The crickets are everywhere. Malcolm finds them in the hay, in the barn, in the chicken coop. The horses whinny in distress, prance and stomp in the corral as if the barn is on fire. Crickets pock the ice on the water trough like frogs skittering about. They hang in the cottonwoods and hedges, and the bare branches squirm in the frigid gray air.

A fence is down and the cattle have scattered.

The sun has barely peeked over the mountains.

Malcolm's breath comes in rapid puffs through clenched teeth. Cold air steams before him like gusts from cannon shot. Even in the frozen air, he smells an alien, acrid odor. And the noise — a billion little buzz saws.

Becky wails from the kitchen and Malcolm knows it has nothing to do with burnt fingers or a cake gone flat.

He runs, feet crunching on the cold ground and cricket bodies.

He finds her, slapping crickets away from piles of fresh herbs lined up by the sink. Her nose wrinkles, pert mouth pinches in disgust, she grunts as she slaps the critters off the counter onto the floor. She dances, stomping them.

"Becky, they're all over —"

Becky looks past Malcolm's shoulder, and her face pales.

He turns to follow her pointed finger at the little black and white TV they kept in the kitchen to entertain her while she cooks or putters with her herbs. Becky likes to hear voices, people talking, even if they don't say anything worth hearing. It's her way of coping with the silence of the Wyoming wilderness. Too far from her folks in Denver. Far, even, from Medicine Bow, the nearest town, especially when it snows for a few days, or the dirt lane out of their isolated little valley turns to mud in the spring.

Becky reads a lot, yes, but she loves that little TV like it was one of the cats.

Crawling in and out of the TV; hundreds of bugs. "Sonsabitches are everywhere," Malcolm screams. "Everywhere." He grabs the TV, oblivious of the bugs on his arms, pulls the cord from the wall socket, and tosses the TV through the window above the sink.

Maybe the shattering glass, or Malcolm's explosive anger, gets to Becky. Her wracking sobs suddenly cease, become rapid gulps as she fights for control. She backhands a few tears off her plump, rosy cheeks and nods her head grimly; she has come to terms. She'd cope.

"It — it was that noise we, we h-heard last night, Mal. They came in the night."

"Those goddam little sonsabitching — "

"Mal." She grabs his arm and he looks at her and his anger suddenly ceases. Time to think. Crisis time, like when the flood hit ten seasons ago and the frost a few years later and that freak hail storm and the range fire last summer. Becky had been his calm, his rock. Like now.

He pats her hand. "I'm all right now." He looks around the kitchen. It isn't as bad as outside. Only a few thousand crickets mill around in the sink and in the cabinets and among Becky's herbs and spice racks lining the counter tops in neat rows of hand-labeled jars. Outside, they hum in their millions a buzz-saw whine that hurts Malcolm's teeth.

"Maybe they like the cold," Malcolm muses.

He looks out the shattered window. Two cats sit on the barn roof looking down, backs arched, tails twitching. "They don't look carnivorous."

"We need to take stock, Mal, protect what food we can."

Malcolm nods. "And water. Let's check the pantry first, see what we can save."

They enter the small room just off the kitchen, lit by a small window at one end facing the just-risen sun. The narrow room is flanked floor to ceiling with shelves on which sit rows of canned goods and jars of preserves and fruit Becky has set aside. Boiling masses of insects glut themselves on flour and sugar sacks on a low shelf. Malcolm tugs his gloves tighter and heaves the bags into the kitchen. Most of the bugs go with the bags.

They close the pantry door, and inside, they stomp and slap till they're certain none remain alive. The door closes too snugly to allow them access. A cold draft exposes a crack in the window where they'd entered. They seal it.

"It's tight," Malcolm pronounces at last. They press duct tape around the window, just in case. "We'll tape the door shut behind us when we go back out."

"We'd better eat now."

Malcolm shakes his head, removes his gloves and tucks them into his belt. "I don't have much of an appetite — "

"When do you figure you'll be really hungry?"

Malcolm smiles. She has her city ways, Becky does, with her TV and her computer and her CB and all, and her books, but she's smart in country ways too.

They sit in the pantry and eat peaches from jars.

"What do you figure?" Malcolm wipes his chin, stifles a burp, and tilts the Mason jar back to drain the juice.

Becky shakes her head. "I don't know."

"I mean, haven't you seen anything on TV? Haven't your CB pals said anything?"

"Nothing on TV. Let's see if the living room set works."

It doesn't. The crickets like wiring insulation. They ate the wiring in the CB too. They mill among the bookshelves thickly.

Becky hangs up the phone. "It's dead."

Malcolm frowns. "We'd better watch out for fire. They could cause a short somewhere."

"I'll hit the fuse box."

They've dealt with outages before. They have a gas generator and they'd eaten by candlelight often enough. They're prepared. They'll get by.

While Becky turns off the power, Malcolm checks the well. The old hand pump works, but the water tastes foul. They can boil the water, if they need to; they have a few water barrels in storage. For emergencies.

Meanwhile, the cricket din fades, as the creatures become a bit more quiescent. Either that, Malcolm thinks, or he's just become more used to the noise.

The thermometer on a post at the front porch says thirty-seven degrees. "Or maybe they do prefer the cold."

Malcolm looks around his farm, his little valley, nestled among deep-forested hills and ridges. The evergreens are giving way to patches of russet and gold among the aspen groves and the alders and oaks as autumn begins to seize the land away from summer. A few banks of early snow cling in gray clumps to rocky stretches high on the ridge a mile to the east. In a few weeks, snow will blanket everything with icy serenity.

The valley doesn't look much different than it does when he was a kid, helping his father raise cows.

Except for the goddam crickets. Everywhere.

Malcolm finds Becky in the living room, warming her hands before a fire in the fireplace.

"Maybe we ought to drive into town," Malcolm says, "see what's going on."

"No." She stands and hugs Malcolm around his paunch, snuggling her head into his shoulder, the smell of wood smoke in her graying hair. "I checked the garage. They got the wiring. And the tires are flat."

"The tires?"

She looks up at him. "Can you believe it? The damn things eat rubber."

Malcolm snorts.

"We could ride in — no, the horses are too skittish. We could walk in, Mal. It's only a few miles."

Malcolm shakes his head. "When they sate themselves, they'll move on."

"Will they?"

"Sure. Most creatures like this do. Mormon crickets, locusts. They all move in cycles. Eat all they can, move on, hibernate, or dig in or whatever they do. Wait another seven years or so and then — bam. Plague, again."

"Most critters, you say?"

"Sure. You remember we had those damn ants once, those little red buggers — "

"These aren't ants, Mal."

He frowns. "You're right. I've never seen the like."

"And it's fall. Don't they do this in the spring?"

They break their clutch and find a dead cricket on the floor. They put it on the kitchen table. Becky brings a magnifying glass she keeps by her herbs.

The creature looks like a Jerusalem cricket, only bigger, more than two inches long. Its thorax is bulbous, honey-brown alternated with black stripes. Its mandibles look like tiny moose antlers jammed into its mouth. Its eyes are huge, glittery, multi-faceted.

With a toothpick, Becky flicks one of the things long hind legs. A tiny tool falls from under it.

The tool looks like a spear, a long blade at one end.

"Jesus H." A trickle of sweat runs down Malcolm's armpit. The room is cold.

Becky pulls strands of dull gray hair back from her forehead and secures them with pins before she bends to her task; an autopsy of a dead — thing.

Under the magnifying glass, on the creature's thorax and abdomen, and on its face, under its eyes and above the mandibles, they see tiny marks. Symbols.

"This looks familiar," Becky muses.

"What?"

"I can't remember."

The spear is a wire. The blade at one end looks like a sliver of glass, tied to the shaft with a strand of a fine material; hair, maybe.

The spear has been secured to the cricket's body in a holster strapped between the thorax and abdomen.

"Jesus H." Malcolm shudders.

"Okay," Becky stands and clutches Malcolm's hand a bit tighter than she intends. He doesn't complain. "It isn't natural, Mal. Whatever it is."

"Then what is it?"

"Some government experiment?"

F.E. Warren Air Force Base, near Cheyenne, is the nearest military installation.

"Nah. They're Air Force at Warren. They used to do missiles there. This kind of thing, maybe out of Utah or those secret places in Nevada, but not here."

"Okay, but what about Laramie? The university."

"I don't know, Becky. I think you'd have seen it on TV or read about it in the papers."

"Then what else? Invasion from outer space?"

Malcolm barks a laugh, relieved at Becky's sense of humor, the strength in her. He doesn't feel so strong.

"Nah. They'd have rayguns, not spears."

"Let's check a few more."

They look at a dozen crickets and find most have symbols painted on their bodies, and most have weapons.

"So they're soldiers. Who are they at war against?"

Malcolm has been studying the milling hordes of crickets in the field beyond the front window of the house while Becky examines cricket corpses. The milling, he decides, has a pattern, beyond instinct, beyond ravenous hunger. The crickets are eating, yes. But they're fighting too. Fighting.

"Look here." He draws Becky to the window and points to the masses of bodies. "They seem to be organized in troops. Look at that mass over there and the one by the cottonwood. About the same size."

Becky catches on. "Yes, and that group by the barn is really two groups. And they're clashing, like a tiny war."

They watch several battles, each composed of thousands, and in some cases, millions, of crickets.

"Huh." Becky clucks her tongue.

"What?"

"Each battle, no matter how big, is paired off almost equally in numbers."

"Yeah, I see what you mean. A dozen battles right here and all of them are about equal. That doesn't make sense."

"And hordes of crickets with tiny spears descending on our farm overnight, making war on each other, does?"

Malcolm snorts. "Okay, right. But if it's only each other they're after, maybe when the battle's over, they'll move on. If that's so, we just wait them out."

"Maybe."

"You got a thought?"

"A couple. One, it doesn't look like anybody's winning, like it's not a matter of one side defeating another."

"I think I follow. We don't know how long they'll fight."

"There's more."

"I'm listening."

"Just a hunch. Let's see what they do with their dead."

They go outside, gloved and booted, and examine a battle on their porch closer. At the front line, where the soldier crickets clash, casualties seem to occur equally. The dead and wounded are lifted by the second line of defenders on each side and passed over to a third line of soldiers, who pass their comrades back further.

At the back of the teeming mass, cricket doctors re-attach severed legs, mandibles, and other body parts. They even put severed heads back on. The apparent dead are re-animated, sent back into the fray.

"Jesus H. I don't see how they're doing it."

"It looks like they just, just — stick the legs back on. Even the heads."

"Not possible. Everything dies, Becky. Everything."

"Mal." Becky touches his arm. His voice has edged toward panic again.

"If they don't die, then what?"

"Mal —"

"Then what, Becky? Then what?"

"Listen, Mal." Becky's grip tightens and Malcolm focuses on her. On the source of his strength. His rock, his calm.

"Okay, Becky. I'm okay."

"The ones inside were corpses. They're dead."

They go back inside and find bodies being hauled out by other crickets, moving in ordered ant-like columns through some access under the sink. They follow the trails and watch the cricket corpses, the ones they'd killed in the house, being repaired, and reanimated.

"Let's burn them, Becky."

They rig torches from Malcolm's welding equipment in the garage and blast bugs. The tang of gasoline replaces the acrid cricket odor. Critters scatter as they stalk the front yard. Black smoke billows in angry mushroom puffs above them into the grayness of the late morning sky before they stop to gauge the result of their attack.

They watch as the critters that had fled their fiery assault slowly return to the fringe of the path they'd blazed. They watch as the crickets gather the charcoaled corpses of their comrades, the few which had been incinerated, and pass the black hulks along to other crickets, to a makeshift cricket hospital a few yards distant.

They watch in horror as the crickets rebuild their comrades. Reanimate them.

"Jesus H." Malcolm retches, bitter orange pulp staining the ground. The crickets converge on the warm feast.

Becky tugs at Malcolm's coat, cooing to him, drawing him away. They leave their makeshift flame-throwers and go back inside. They sit at the kitchen table. Malcolm wipes bile from his lips and spits on the floor.

Becky does not complain. She finds a jar of tea in the fridge and pours two glasses. "Food in the fridge is okay, but we'd better eat it if we're going to keep the power off too long."

"We should leave." Malcolm's voice sounds strangled.

"They're quieter. A bit."

"I think it might be the temperature. I think they like it cold." He gulps the tea and sighs. "We should still leave, walk into town. See what's going on elsewhere."

"Or we could go as far as the Beckwith's. Maybe they know something. Maybe the crickets are only here."

"What if they're everywhere?"

"Maybe. Maybe not." Becky stands, resolute. "A three mile hike will do us good."

Malcolm stands, mute, glum.

He loads the twelve-gauge and stuffs shells in his pockets as they set out. Becky hefts a backpack; Malcolm has no idea what it holds, but she always takes it with her when she hikes the woods in the spring and summer looking for herbs.

As they leave, Malcolm notices the collapsed corral fence. Sometime during the fiery skirmish in the front yard, the horses broke out, scattered.

They find the going easy along the hard-packed dirt road that rises and falls among the hills and vales just outside their lit-tle valley. The crickets still sing their buzz saw chorus among the leaves blanketing the forest floor on either side of the road, but as the sun climbs higher in the gunmetal gray sky, the humming quiets even more.

The Beckwith place is empty. Crickets, everywhere.

Malcolm calls into the open front door of the log house, shotgun cocked and ready. No answer. Becky checks the barn, where she finds the horses gone, and two saddles missing from their pegs. Then she joins Malcolm, looking around the house.

"Mal," she calls from the dining room. "Come see."

Malcolm obliges. Becky stands over the Beckwith's dining table, where John and Doris Beckwith had not long ago performed an autopsy of the crickets just as Becky had done.

They see cricket parts on the tablecloth. A magnifying glass lay there, and scissors, pins and other things.

And a book lay open.

Becky looks at the big book and a smaller notebook by it. Symbols.

She picks up the book, which smells of mildew and dust, and reads. "The History of Magical Manifestations, by Montague Winters, 1925."

"Magic?" Malcolm studies the symbols in the notebook, done in Doris' blocky script. "These symbols are magic?"

"They're like some on the crickets we took apart."

"Magic?"

Becky shrugs. "Doris was into magic. She was Wiccan." She begins poking through Doris' shelves, pulling books down, and stacking them on the table.

"I don't know, Becky." Malcolm sits heavily in John's chair at the table, arms folded in front of his hanging head. "I might buy a scientific experiment going cock-eyed, almost. I can maybe even believe in an invasion from —"

Becky stops pulling books from shelves and looks at Malcolm, fists anchored on wide hips. "You saw the symbols. I told you they looked familiar. I remember now. I saw them last time I visited Doris. She's into herbs too, but not as much as I am. And she's Wiccan, like I said, but I'm not into the craft like she is. Anyway, I'll bet she knows something we don't. Or she did."

Malcolm blinks, takes a deep breath, then nods and stands. "I'll help you gather books."

"Just help me carry them. I'm not sure what to look for."

In a few minutes, they decide against taking the books back to their house. They'll stay at the Beckwith's and study there. John and Doris will understand, when they come back.

"If there are no crickets in Laramie," Malcolm says, "John and Doris'll be back with the goddam army. If there are —"

The Beckwith's have a cellular phone, but they can't find it. The power is off and the trucks, both of them, won't start. The tires are flat.

The fridge is full.

By late afternoon, as it warms, the crickets grow almost silent, their buzz a background hiss.

As night descends and the land refreezes with the setting sun, the cricket activity picks up again and their oddly even battle rages on.

Malcolm and Becky eat by the crackling light and warmth of the fireplace, cuddle in wool blankets on a large sofa. The

crickets keep out of the well-insulated house; Beckwith has done a better job insulating his home than has Malcolm. They are able to eat, rest, and study in relative peace.

Many of the books in Doris' collection are in Latin, Greek, French and other languages. Becky reads some French. Most are in English. They read, into the night. Becky finds evidence of something — magical.

"A magical war?" Malcolm shakes his head. "You're saying some magician, some wizard, is engaged in a magical —"

"Yes, with some other wizard. Or group. They're using these crickets. They're manifestations of their powers, you see, the crickets. They've been conjured up to engage in —"

"Was Doris involved?"

Becky thinks for a moment. "No, I don't think so. But maybe — I, I don't know."

"Why here? Why us?"

Becky holds Malcolm's sweaty hand. "I'm beginning to think they're not just in the Medicine Bow Mountains, Mal. They're everywhere. Like you said. Everywhere."

Malcolm's skin crawls, as if infested with crickets. "What can we do?"

"Maybe this kind of magic, once turned loose, has to run its course. That's what I'm getting from what I read, bits and pieces. You saw how the crickets resurrected each other, put each other back together, like machine parts. Maybe that isn't far-fetched. Maybe it's truth."

"So they're machines. Magical machines. They can't die. They can't be killed."

Becky shrugs, tight-lipped.

"What do we do, Becky?"

"Maybe we just wait till the magic wears off."

"Wears off?"

"Runs out of gas. The batteries wear out. Whatever. Mal, this takes power of some kind."

"The crickets quiet down when it gets warm. They could stay active till spring."

"It could take that long."

"Jesus H. We'll have to find a way to survive till then."

They take stock. They have enough food put by at their own place, food the crickets won't get to, to last a few weeks. They might be able to hunt, but they'll have to do that soon. The crickets are eating all the grasses and other foliage. The animals might starve for want of forage.

If the Beckwith's don't return, they have some food there. A few more weeks.

There's no point in going farther afield. The cities, even little Medicine Bow, will be empty, or a wasteland of starving, desperately fighting people, trying to survive.

Goddam crickets, everywhere.

"No, we have to find a way to kill them, Becky. We can't outlast them. Can't count on it. We could starve first."

"But they can't be killed."

"Maybe we can find the ones doing this, get them to stop."

"Maybe even they can't stop it."

"Keep reading." Malcolm helps Becky study.

"Some of this stuff is so, so — bizarre," he says. Dust from one old book tickles his nose and he sneezes. "Old, too."

"Doris never showed me but a few of her books. This one," Becky thumps one book with crisp, yellowed pages, "written in 1650–something. In Latin. Can't help us much."

In time, sleep overtakes Becky. Malcolm reads on in candlelight as Becky snores a soft counterpart to the buzz from the warring magical crickets outside.

He finds a passage in one book, a handwritten note in an upper corner of a stained, torn page, in a crimped spastic hand, some of it in French. Something about a kind of power, its use and abuse. And a warning.

Malcolm strains to read the arcane passage. In time, his eyes grow tired and he sleeps.

In the morning, he awakes to the scent of coffee. And something burning, like game meat, a bit over-cooked. It isn't elk, deer or antelope. Not moose. Beaver?

He stands and stretches creaking bones. He tosses another log onto the low fire and pads, barefoot, into the bathroom to relieve himself. Outside the frosted bathroom window, a light snow has started to fall, a sparkling mist in the slanted early morning light. The cricket wars wage on and on.

"The cold, all right," Malcolm mutters. "Turns the little bastards on."

He goes to the kitchen and finds Becky humming to herself, a smile forming crinkles around her eyes. She stands over the old wood-burning stove, stirring something fragrant in a large cauldron with a wooden spoon.

"Haven't seen you smile since the day before yesterday." He gives her a peck on the cheek.

"Coffee's on," she says, nodding at the pot. Malcolm finds a cup and pours. He sits at the table.

"The crickets will quiet down, I reckon, by noon," he says. "Do you think we ought to walk back to our place?"

"Maybe. There's still some things I need to look up in Doris' books. Meanwhile —" Becky turns from the stove and holds out the wooden spoon, a hand cupped beneath it to catch drips. "Taste this." She brings the spoon to Malcolm.

"What is it?" Malcolm sniffs the gamy brew, takes the spoon from Becky, and licks at the milky, reddish contents.

"A little tomato, oregano, carrots —"

"A stew?"

"And for the meat —"

Malcolm sputters and spits, suddenly realizing what he just swallowed. "You're kidding." He wipes his chin.

Becky laughs, bosom shaking. "Don't they taste good?"

"Hell, Becky, you could make — magical crickets — taste good." Malcolm licks the wooden spoon clean, rises and goes to the stove. He dips up another spoonful and nibbles.

"Hm," he says at last. "Tastes like chicken."

Becky joins his laughter and they eat together, cricket stew for breakfast, with orange juice, toast, and coffee.

"We'll be okay, Mal." She hugs him. His rock, his calm. "We'll outlast these little demons."

Malcolm feels suddenly queasy. It isn't the stew; something he'd dreamed last night; no, something he read before he dozed off. "Becky, I want you to look at something."

She follows him into the dining room. On the floor, by the sofa, the book lay open to the page he'd been reading.

"What does this say?" Malcolm points to the odd passage. "Something about power. And I think this is a warning. I can't make it all out. It is partly in French."

"My French is not too good, but — " Becky takes the book, sits and reads. In a moment, her lips begin to move as she whispered along with the words on the yellowed page. In a moment, her hands begin to tremble.

"Becky?"

In a moment, she begins to weep. Huge gulping sobs.

"Becky?" He kneels on the floor and hugs Becky, her violent sobs shaking them both. His rock, his calm.

"What is it, Becky? What?"

In time, a long time, her sobs subside enough for her to tell him about the power of the sun, how it can be magically har-nessed to animate something like the crickets. In time, she is able to read the passage, most of it, aloud, a warning.

"They get their power from the sun," she explains. "They're tapping it. Like a battery. Draining it."

After a moment, Malcolm walks out to the kitchen to check the thermometer sitting just outside the window above the sink. A dusting of snow caps the thermometer. Malcolm wipes away a film of frost and reads the mercury.

He shudders.

He walks back into the living room. "I'll chop some wood this afternoon," he says.

He puts another log on the fire and sits by his wife on the sofa, putting one arm around her. She weeps quietly and Malcolm just holds her, patting her shoulder, rocking back and forth.

His wife. His rock. His calm. 𝄇

Ken Rand resides with his family in Utah, where he writes semi-full-time. He's sold fifty-plus to Weird Tales *and some fifty other magazines and anthologies. Books published include* The 10% Solution: Self-editing for the Modern Writer *(Fairwood Press) and* Tales from the Lucky Nickel Saloon *(Yard Dog Press). His website: www.sfwa.org/members/Rand.*

The Nightmare Avatar's Nightmare

BY MIKE ALLEN & CHRISTINA SNG

Along the alley wall
it crawls, spiderlike
and grotesque, face
like a child's, a murdered
child's, swollen and black
with coagulated blood;

It smiles, teeth sharp
as ice slivers formed
on remote mountains
where hearts and corpses
remain as cold as its
eyes which glisten like

icicles in the stormchoked
night, where it climbs
without fear or slippage,
tiny hands at the tips of
each limb clasping silently
as it lowers itself onto

a balcony where the
scent of prey is thick,
a child whose fears are
ripe for manifesting,
who presses her pale face
hard against the screen

and grins toothily at
the dismayed visage
before her, staring with
unblinking feral eyes.
No fear clouds her mind,
no joy, no dreams, save

a hunger in her gaze
that echoes its own,
her soul parched, stunted,
starved even of nightmares.
Her visitor turns and flees
into the sewer below

as welts open in its shadowy
flesh, fear crescendoing,
rapturous hunger uncoiling;
with no nightmares to harvest
but its own, the abyssal
famine consumes from within,

leaving nothing
but a shell
of black dream dust,
banished with a laugh,
a cough,
an apathetic sigh. 𝄇

Nine Little Demons

(OUT OF ALMOST 100 CONJURED VIA PEN AND RANDOM-NAME GENERATOR)

by Ben Towle

ABAS

ADRAX

AGARBAS

AHRIR

ALLUS

AMDUSION

AZARAX

BALLOS

BAROBAS

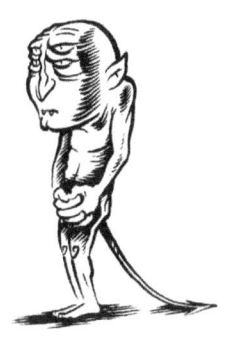

Ever

by Jay Lake

You meet a certain class of people on the bus. Short, dark men who slop floors and work harder than I ever will for a fraction the money. Tired women with hard eyes and sad mouths, dark roots in their hopeful blonde hair. Guys having intense conversations with grocery bags, reporting in minute detail on their progress through the streets of Portland.

Me, I'm big with a beard, so most people leave me alone. When the bus gets crowded, someone will finally slip in next to me, avoiding eye contact though we're arm-to-arm and thigh-to-thigh, closer together than my wife and I sleep at night. There's a weird, jostling intimacy, like dry-humping as high school freshmen, except your elbow gets all the action, and the stranger walks away without a word.

Until one day this little guy sits down next to me, and it's like someone set a theatre lamp on the bus. You can't help but stare into the spotlight. There wasn't much to see — rumpled suit, purple satin with orange threaded needlework, like Emmett Kelly in street drag, little wire glasses my Granddaddy might have mislaid fifty years ago, and drowning pool eyes. I looked at him, and if he hadn't laughed, I'd still be on that bus as some weird piece of transit art, the Transfiguration of the Commuter.

But laugh he did, and I could hear forests bloom to life in the peal of his voice. It was like Mt. Hood laughing, as if the Columbia River had noticed me. I smiled into the force of his mirth, my lips stretching almost against their will.

"Hey, Jay," he said. There was a tiny swipe of mustard at one side of his mouth, and he had garlic on his breath, but that was okay with me. If all the turf farms in the Willamette Valley had lungs, they would not have smelled half so sweet.

"Um, hi." I was still pulled toward his eyes, but the fact that he knew my name flooded me with pleasure, a virtual orgasm of the soul. Even the hissing of the bus' airbrakes was a choir.

He laid his left hand on my elbow. Through three layers of clothing, I felt the spark. My arm was warm, my skin prickling. "I've got an offer," he said. "Once in a lifetime."

"Yes," I whispered. I would follow this man anywhere.

He laughed again, squeezing my arm. "Maybe you should hear me out first."

"Yes." Suddenly I was ashamed of my eagerness.

Leaning close, his breath was hot upon my face, a forest fire on the green slopes of the mountain. His voice dropped, so that all the bus people watching us couldn't overhear. "Want to live forever?"

I don't believe in God, as far as I know He doesn't believe in me. I don't believe in afterlife or reincarnation or any of those things. But I believed in this little man in the rumpled purple suit the way I believed in the beating of my own heart.

I've never understood the curse of the Wandering Jew. Ahasuerus' fate always seemed to me to be a reward. To watch the march of history, to see every sun set from now until the end of time — these would be the richest gifts a man could ask. Witness the building of cities on the moon. Travel to the stars. I smiled, my lips moved, I began to say "yes, yes," to leap from my seat, then I stopped.

My daughter waited for me at home, my wife, everything in my life — bills, email, books unread, stories unwritten, meals uneaten, dirty clothes, empty toilet paper rolls. The march of days, ordinary as ever they were.

"Next stop," he said, reaching across me to tug the cord. "Make up your mind."

I might someday bury my wife. If I lived forever, I would someday bury my daughter. And her daughters.

The bus shuddered to a halt, the lamp of his presence went out, and the little man smiled a crooked smile and shuffled off into forever. I pressed my head against the cold glass and whispered my troubles into the fog of my breath until the bus took me home to love. ◑

Jay Lake lives in Portland, Ore., and is the author of over 200 short stories as well as novels from Tor Books, Night Shade Books and Fairwood Press. Jay can be reached via his website: www.jlake.com.

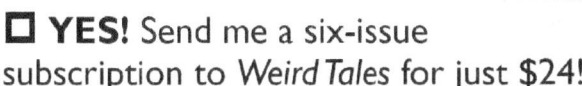

The Old Ones Reborn

by Erin Donahoe

I. The Book

It all began because I was not afraid
and I told the bookseller so.
Horror tales never disturbed me
never elicited that much desired chill of terror.
His eyes lit with a malign light
and he excused himself for many long moments
in the musty and ill lit chambers
he kept behind the store front.
He returned, a dark desperation limning his face,
with a heavy, filthy tome, covered in the dirt of ages
which he hefted onto the counter with affected lugubriousness.
He instructed me to wait until the next full moon
and then, only then, should I open the book
and begin to read.

If only I had realized then.

Those Old Ones, Timeless Ones, Ancient Ones,
that exist between our own
sparkling facets of reality
can be infinitely patient, infinitely vigilant
waiting for their time at the top of the wheel
to re-turn.
I had taken the bookseller's recommendation
with a laugh, unconcerned at the time
by the repeated smacking of his lips
or his lustful glee held barely in check.
I thought merely that very few

H. P. LOVECRAFT'S MAGAZINE OF HORROR

of his customers must be women.
I did not know how eagerly those forgotten
(never gone, never gone, never really forgotten)
Ones would grasp for their objective,
and in my quaint thoughts of the eerie trait
reading in the light of the gibbous moon would impart,
it never occurred to me that the night of the full moon
was a night of fertility.

II. The Reading

I lifted the heavy tome
and placed it on the table before the window
moonlight shining in upon the book's
dark surface.
The cover was leathery, the hide of some
rough and unknown creature.
Words, barely legible, were raised on the
front of the codex, written in a tongue
I did not understand. I had explained to the bookseller
that I could not read Latin. He seemed amused,
and assured me I would have no problem
reading this text.

We were about to see.

I lit three candles, in assistance to the moonlight
as per the bookseller's instruction,
and I felt a thrill of anticipation.
Even were the contents of the book only mediocre,
unable to frighten me,
at least the theatrics were good ~ I would need
to thank the instigator.
(Little did I realize, then, how thorough
a thanking he would get.)
I reached down to open the book
and a tingle rushed up my arm, a dark
spectrum of color splashed before my eyes
some eldritch magic of times long gone by.
And then there was nothing.

III. The Dream

My explanation at the time was
that it was some kind of hypnosis, that I was sleepwalking.
I only remember feeling that I had been submerged
in warm, nearly scalding water, but that,
in some manner, I was able
to breathe.
There were light touches all over my body
though I cannot swear they were human appendages exploring me
and I know that something entered me, came into me

in the ways humans do
but by what shrouded epithelium I was desecrated
I can only give hypotheses, as you will see.
I know at that point I tried to scream
and writhed to no avail.

Perhaps I should be thankful that is all I can recall.

I woke on the beach, naked and alone,
the sand sticking to my skin, a harsh, abrasive balm,
that I greeted with relief, glad to be on land.
I was not yet free from the terror of my dream,
if it was, indeed, a dream, which I no longer believe.
It was night, though the moon must have already set,
and the stars shone cold and distant, winking in a way
that made me shiver.
I slipped through the darkness, hoping that no one
would witness my nocturnal wanderings,
thankful that I recognized my surroundings well enough
to make my way home.
I slipped into my house, my door fortuitously unlocked, unbolted,
to see the three candles extinguished, burned to
pools of wax upon my table.
The book was nowhere to be found.
Nor were my clothes.

IV. The Visions

The things I saw over the next several days,
and so many days since,
were terrifying in ways mere words
could never describe or explain;
but minding that inadequacy, I will attempt
to tell here of the most prominent
of my visions.
Vision. It seems such a soft word,
innocuous at best,
it is the first of my imperfect terms,
used to describe the all consuming display
of images and emotions that would overcome me,
leaving me in a trancelike state, filled
with a revelation of the future
that no Delphic oracle, no fortune telling gypsy,
nay, no pope or bishop could ever transcend.

May God have mercy on my soul, if I should have one left.

In this particular ocular, auditory, and olfactory adventure,
I am standing at the top of a rocky spire,
looking down at the sea below me
as it bubbles and churns menacingly
spewing forth sulfurous fumes that mix
with the scent of brine.

There is a horrible, earth-rending wail
as if the ground beneath the water
were crying out in agony.
More than once I have come back to myself,
the wide eyes of strangers staring,
their gaping mouths telling me that I had been screaming.
They do not know what I know, what I fear most:

In this vision, I am pregnant.

V. The End(?)

I stand here at last,
as I have foretold, an unknown
and uncelebrated Nostradamus,
cursing the accuracy of my own predictions.
The sea below me is indeed teeming
with some hereto undiscovered terror,
and I now admit completely that I
am most definitely afraid.
Already, though, I can see the minute
but multitudinous differences between my vision
and the reality before me.
I am not alone on this rocky pedestal;
the bookseller is here with me,
the gleam in his eye telling me
that while he may not be the father of the
burden in my womb
he certainly had the pleasure
of violating me.

I do not remember how I came to stand here.

I may not recall entirely the past,
yet I can see the moment coming:
a nexus of possible futures;
a convergence of untold aeons;
a split second of time pregnant in more
than the conventional sense.
My belly laces with a contraction
and I know the time has come.
I look down the sharp and jutting slope
that extends cliff-like below me
in a fashion I know is deadly, and try
to work against the implacable lethargy,
to preserve all of humanity . . .
to jump.

If you are wise, you will pray for me,
whatever Gods you call on.

I will take all the help I can get . ⟲

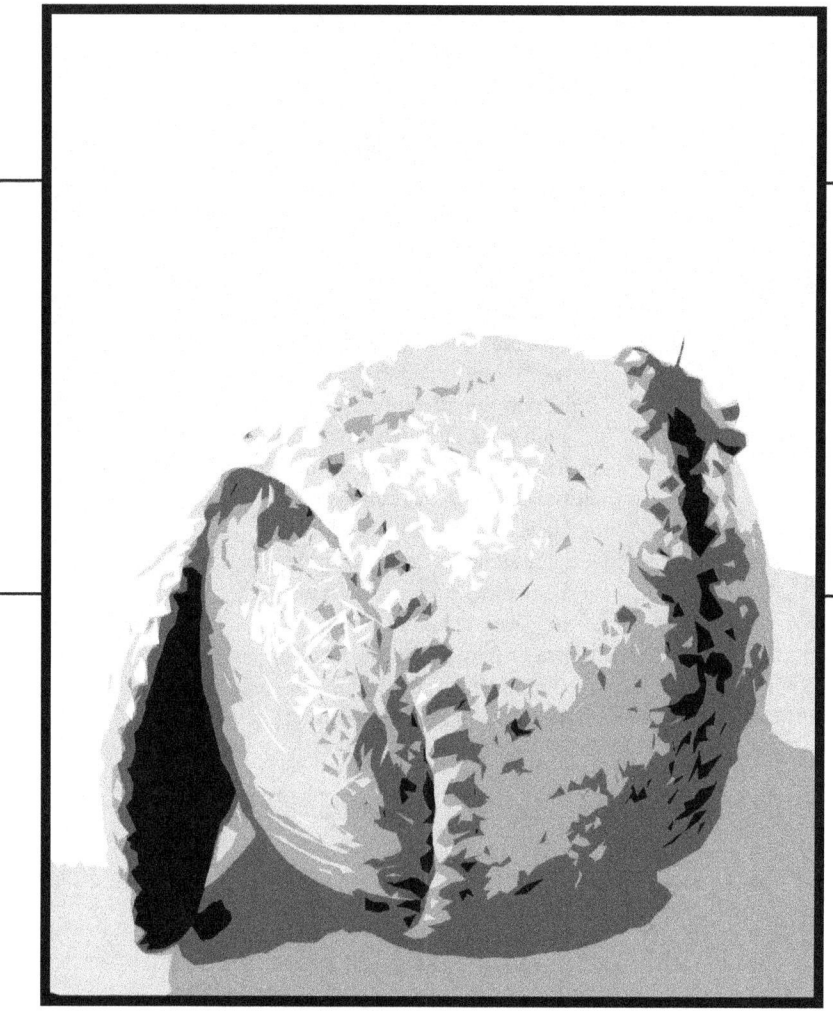

ILLUSTRATION BY O'JAY BARBEE

THE OLD MAN JUST
WANTED THE BOY
TO BE HAPPY.

The Taxidermist's Collection

by Toiya Finley

I t's been 10 o'clock for the past three hours. During that time, the Smiths' yard went through four complete seasons, and the creek out back boiled to tar. The Smiths' boy hides in the closet. He sprinted off before the baseball hit the glass. But Sandy Jenkins, Greg Tate, and Roger Black aren't hiding in the bellies of their houses like Quinn. The leaves in their front yards haven't withered to ash and the earth hasn't split, even though Roger Black threw the pitch, Sandy set up the teams, and Greg asked Quinn to play. Old Man Johnson's only interested in Quinn Smith. He's the one who sent the ball shooting through the window.

The Smiths have no chance of paying off Old Johnson, which is why their car just fell in a heap in the driveway. Both lost their jobs when the shoe factory closed down. Problem is, they've got no idea what Old Man Johnson could want. He never comes out of his house, and no one knows if he's still alive until something happens—like today—in the neighborhood.

By the sixth 10 AM hour, all the food in the refrigerator's spoiled to mush. Crumbs spill from the cabinets. No sense in getting the police involved. Their canines went rabid and chewed off some rookie's leg last time they intervened. Daddy Smith notices the house is on tilt. All the furniture in the den slid across the floor and smacked against the wall. Pretty soon—maybe the eighth or ninth 10 o'clock hour—the whole house will slip into that widening hole in the earth.

"Quinn, can you come out a second?" Mama Smith's the one to deliver the news, her and Daddy deciding now's a good time. All the silver's melted in the

drawers, and the mirrors have turned back to sand. "Go on over to Old Man Johnson's. See what he wants."

The boy emerges from the closet, knowing there ain't another way to deal with the present problem. But he knows that if his parents had finished high school, maybe had better jobs, the money could've been sent to the old man. That would've been the end of it.

Quinn stumbles down the now crooked stairs following his mama. His daddy stands at the back door tall and grim. The Smiths watch the boy leave in shocked silence, knowing this must certainly be their son's death march.

Instead of hurtling the gulf of flames in the front yard, Quinn hops the tar creek and makes his way across the field to Old Man Johnson's. All of a sudden, it's twilight outside, and somewhere off on a distant street, kids are riding their bikes and laughing.

Old Man Johnson's got a collection, Quinn heard. A whole collection of stuffed boys lined up in a row, like dead owls and bobcats propped up at the museum. Quinn figured, back while he was in the deep recesses of the closet, Old Man Johnson would want him for the collection. A stuffed boy for a broken window doesn't make a whole lot of a sense to Quinn, but then adults are strange people.

"That you, Quinn Smith?" Old Man Johnson's voice is high and withered behind the door.

"Unh huh." Quinn shakes on the porch and wonders what it's like to be stuffed full of cotton balls.

"Who sent you? Your ma ma?" he says, like Quinn's got two mothers.

"Unh huh. I didn't mean to break your window, Mr. Johnson. I can get an allowance somehow. I can pay you back."

"Oh, Quinn Smith, I got all the money I need. I got too much money."

Ain't too much money to have, as far as Quinn Smith is concerned.

"I gotta better idea, Quinn Smith. I'm an ooooold man. I been in this body a-hundred-n-five years. That's a mighty long time."

Quinn agrees.

"I've done great things in all those years. I've had a lot of fun. But when a body grows old, Quinn Smith, it gets run down. It don't work to well anymore. I wish I was young again. I like being young."

"I'm sorry. What do you want? We can't pay for the window. Please don't make our house disappear. Please don't hurt my parents."

"That wouldn't be quite right, seein' as they didn't break my window. We can come up with somethin', can't we?"

Quinn imagines the cotton balls clogging up his throat. He coughs real hard like when he's all sweaty and his mouth's dry. He doesn't want to know how that feels—being stuffed with cotton balls for 105 years. "Please don't stuff me, Mr. Johnson!"

Old Man Johnson laughs. He's not mad at all. "We can make a deal, Quinn Smith. You do want lots of money, don't ya?"

Quinn Smith nods his head real hard. There won't be a new factory opening up in this town any time soon, and Mama and Daddy will stay on the couch in the den sippin' beer. The holes in Quinn's shirt will grow, there'll never be money for college, and he'll end up trapped here with his parents.

"Oh, yessir! I want lots of money!"

The Smiths don't expect their son home so soon. They didn't expect him to come home at all. But he walks through the door, and the house rights itself. The clock says it's 7 PM.

"Everything's okay!" The boy grins.

Well, obviously, Daddy and Mama think, it is. Mama finds the macaroni shells are no longer dust, and everything's right in the refrigerator. "It's not spoiled! We can even have cheese with the macaroni. Does that sound good, Quinn?"

He nods and can't wait to eat macaroni and cheese again. Being poor ain't a concern for him, now that he's got this young body. Johnson looks out from Quinn's eyes and grins. Old Quinn's got his money now, so it's a fair trade. That body is good for another twenty years. Quinn won't spend all that money in twenty years.

Johnson sits down to dinner with the Smiths, eager to start this new life. Once Old Quinn's dead, Johnson'll move back into the house and set the old husk of a body he was in just a few minutes ago in line with all the other old husks.

"We're sorry, son, we had to send you up there," Daddy Smith says. "We're glad everything worked out for you."

Johnson stuffs his mouth with macaroni and cheese. "You don't have to worry. Everything always works out for me." ↻

Nashville native Toiya Kristen Finley is a freelancer who was a professional student in another life. Her fiction has appeared in Text: UR — The New Book of Masks, Not One of Us, Tales of the Unanticipated, TEL: Stories, Darker Matter, *and* The Nine Muses. *Upcoming work will appear in* GrendelSong *and* New Writings in the Fantastic. *She is the founding and former managing/fiction editor of* Harpur Palate.

Nine More Demons

(OUT OF ALMOST 100 CONJURED VIA PEN AND RANDOM-NAME GENERATOR)

by Ben Towle

BEELICAS

BEELL

BEERIR

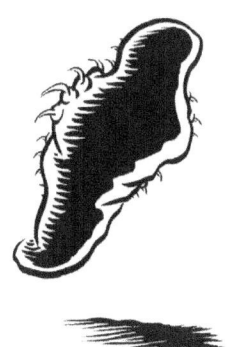

BERS

CERBAS

CIMODEUS

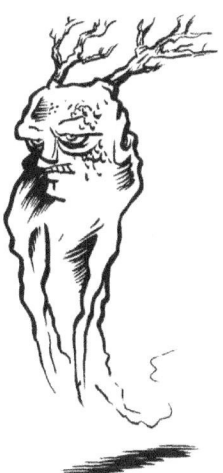

DAIME

DAITH

DAITZITH

ILLUSTRATION BY PETER MIHAICHUK

HE WAS A GOD, SEE.
AN ALIEN OCTOPUS GOD.
AND HE WAS NO DAMN GOOD.

The Really Big Sleep

by Esther Friesner

I knew she was trouble the minute she ankled into my office. For one thing, she didn't have any ankles. Not a whole lot left of her calves either, just a pair of raw and bleeding stumps, though I glimpsed some pretty sweet leftover kneecaps peeking out from under that tight red skirt. She must've had a killer pair of gams, once upon a time.

Yeah, I looked her over. You call it sexist, I call it on-the-job bennies. The pay stinks in this business; I take my perks where I can. The name's Dalos, Tim Dalos. I'm a detective and it's a dog's life.

The babe caught me ogling her gnawed-off pins and smiled.

"Like what you see?" she purred in a voice as sweet as peaches and arsenic, hitching up her skirt a couple more inches to show off skin white as the icy plateau of Leng. She floated in mid-air in front of my desk like a bubble of marsh-gas on the surface of a swamp, her curves giving off a green-litten necrotic light. On her it looked good.

I decided to play it cool. Never let them see you sweat, that's my motto. Sweat or drool. Sweat, drool, or dance naked around a black monolith in the woods. Sweat, drool, dance naked or — well, you get the idea.

"I've seen better," I said, tilting back my fedora and pretending that the temperature in the room hadn't gone up ten degrees.

She pursed her lips and frowned. Talk about the big chill. She could give lessons to the ice in my breakfast whiskey. "I doubt you'd say that if you'd seen me about a week ago," she said. "P.S."

"P.S.?" I echoed.

"Pre-shoggoth." She shimmered closer and got a little altitude, so that the stumps of her missing legs hovered above my desk. Good thing I'd bought a new blotter last Sabbat; those things were still dripping. I dabbled my index finger in one of the bigger droplets and sniffed: 45% blood, 35% ichor, 15% My Sin and 5% hers. There was more to this dame than met the eye.

I gave her stems a close inspection, but not close enough to earn myself a slap in the face. Don't listen to that crowd of gibbering jerks down at Howard's Bar and Grill; I can act like a pro even when I'm dealing with a gorgeous woman.

"That's a shoggoth bite, all right," I said at last. "Nasty one, too. You're lucky to be alive. If you are."

"Oh, I assure you, Mr. Dalos, I am very much alive," she replied. "Alive and angry. That's why I'm here." She reached into her purse and whipped out a wad of green thick enough to choke the Black Goat of the Woods and every last one of its Thousand Young. That settled the whole dead-or-alive question as far as I was concerned: The dead don't cough up retainers.

You don't want to know what the dead do cough up; trust me on this.

"That's a lot of dough, sister," I remarked, still not touching it. I didn't know where it had been. "You might as well know up front that I'm a shamus, not a

hitman. I don't do contract killings; strictly freelance, work-for-hire. If you want revenge — "

"How perceptive of you." She gave me the Mona Lisa treatment. "Of course I want revenge, but don't worry about your precious reputation as an honourable P.I. The pleasures of direct retribution will be all mine. I wouldn't have it any other way. All I need you to do for me, Mr. Dalos, is hunt down the shoggoth that did this to me; hunt it down and bring it to my home. Alive."

A crisp, white calling card materialized like a bill collector, out of nowhere, and wafted down to join the bale of shekels on my desk. I picked it up and read it, then whistled, long and low. The copperplate Gothic engraving said Vera Whately and the address was in a part of town so posh that the dogs used social secretaries to set up their butt-sniffing appointments. I knew the Whately name — who didn't? It was a name that screamed old blood and old shipping money. It screamed a lot of other things too, usually "Iä! Iä! C'thulhu f'thagn!" down by the docks on the night of the full moon.

While I was still giving her card the once-over, Miss Whately backed off to let me have some breathing room. I looked up just in time to see her sprout a fresh, unmangled, drop-dead gorgeous pair of stems as she drifted back to the floor.

"Cute trick," I remarked. "But can you do the one with the weasel, the feathers, and the gallon jug of honey?"

She wrinkled her nose at me and straightened her skirt. "I'm not paying you to be crude, Mr. Dalos."

"Too bad. You'd get your money's worth." I swung my feet onto the desktop and lit up. Then I put down the whiskey glass and got out a cigarette. "I'll be frank with you, dollface," I told her. "You say you want revenge, but for what? You just made that shoggoth bite go bye-bye faster than a Hollywood marriage. You're none the worse for wear, so why spend a bundle of lettuce for my services?"

"Au contraire, Mr. Dalos," she said, her pale green eyes narrowing. "Something did happen: A shoggoth bit me. Do you realize what that means?"

"Bad shoggoth, no biscuit?" I suggested.

Apparently some people don't care much for the old Tim Dalos trademarked boyish charm. Without warning, something hit me with the force of a tidal wave, smashing into my chest and hurling me heels over head out of my chair, through the office wall, and out into the hallway beyond. Salt water stung my eyes, seaweed went up my nose, lights exploded inside my skull and herring got personal up my trousers. That was when I realized that what had hit me like a tidal wave was a tidal wave. Not a big one, but big enough to peeve my landlord.

I was still coughing up anchovies when Miss Whately stepped daintily through the broken wall. The power that allowed her to regenerate limbs like a starfish stopped short of letting her conjure up new shoes to fit 'em, so she was treading her barefooted way carefully through a minefield of splintered furniture and lumps of broken plaster.

"I really should have warned you, Mr. Dalos," she said. "When faced with the possibility of becoming a murder victim, we Whatelys are not known for having a sense of humour."

"Murder?" I wrung brine from my fedora.

"Murder, Mr. Dalos," she repeated. "Murder, not so pure and far from simple." She offered me one slender hand to help me to my feet, but she didn't let me hold onto it a second longer than necessary. It felt soft and smooth, like really pricey lox. "Someone wants me dead."

"Someone who doesn't know you too well, if they thought you'd bleed to death from that shoggoth bite," I said.

"Or someone who knows me quite well," she countered. "Someone who wants me to be aware that they are working towards my death; someone who wants me to agonize over it while they savour my fear. Only when my distress no longer entertains them will they deliver the coup de grâce. That was just a warning shoggoth."

She sounded pretty sure of herself. I knew better than to be sure of anything, in this business. "Any idea why anyone'd want you dead?" I asked her.

She shrugged. "I'm the sole heir to the Hezekiah Whately shipping fortune, Chairman of the Board for Innsmouth Gas and Eclectic, President of Wendigo Logging, Pulp and Paper, and the most successful Amway rep you ever saw. I've made my share of enemies, some of them out of the spare parts I had left over from previous enemies. If I had a nickel for every toe I ever stepped on, I'd have two million, eight hundred sixty-five thousand, nine hundred eighty-three dollars and twenty-seven cents."

"At a nickel a toe?" I scratched my head. It didn't add up. "Sister, I hope you hired good accountants for your companies, because you don't know math."

"Or you don't know the peculiar sort of toes I manage to step on, Mr. Dalos," she replied. "My first husband alone managed to have twenty-nine."

"An over-achiever, huh?" So was she, judging by the way she said first husband. I tried to scope out her hands on the q.t. No sign of a wedding ring.

"That's right, Mr. Dalos: I'm not currently married." Apparently I was going to have to take a brush-up course in Stealth 101. "But thank you for checking so discreetly. I appreciate old-fashioned gallantry. After six husbands, I think I'd better try life as a bachelor girl for a while, at least until I get my strength back." She gave me a wicked wink and I felt my heart drop into the yawning abyss between the stars.

I shook it off. Focus, Tim, focus, I told myself. You don't get paid for playing Hide the Unspeakable Basalt Figurine of Arcane Design with the clients. More's the pity. "Six ex-husbands is quite a past, sister. Any chance one of them's the one who tried to say it with shoggoths?"

She leaned in close. Her lips were full, moist, and more tempting than an all-expense-paid trip to Unknown Kadath. Her eyes held the exotic mysteries of the sea, and the warm, intoxicating scent of her ripe, willing body made my head spin. "You tell me," she murmured right before she kissed me.

When she finally walked out of my ruined office, I picked the last few chunks of fallen plaster out of my bleeding back, got dressed and got to work.

A few phone calls cleared Vera's exes: Five out of the six were dead and the last one was touring Japan as a Judy Garland impersonator. I needed a new lead and I needed it fast. That meant there was just one place to go: Pickman's. Pickman's is an artsy little place down in the Tenderloin district, but there's nothing tender about the meat on sale inside. You tell me what makes an ordinary Joe decide he's going to leave the wife and kids at home and take a walk on the wild side. Once they go to Pickman's, they stop walking and just crawl. It's down in the gutter, which makes it Number One for picking up the word on the street.

I found Pickman himself tending bar, just like always. Word on the street had it that he'd once been the golden boy of the NYU film school, only he decided film didn't count as real art, so he'd shucked lenses for linseed oil, cameras for canvas, and an obnoxiously pretentious attitude for ... Well okay, maybe some things don't change. The trouble was, when he burned all his celluloid bridges behind him and leaped into the world of Art, he forgot one little detail: He couldn't paint worth a damn. He claimed it was because he just hadn't found the right model yet.

I sat down at the bar between a girl and a ghoul and got

Pickman's attention by unfolding a fifty. He was on me faster than gore on guts. "Long time no see, Dalos," he said by way of greeting. "What'll you have?"

"Information," I said. "On the rocks. With a twist."

Pickman scowled. "What's it look like, I'm running a library? Take a hike, shamus."

"Maybe later. Right now my dogs are killing me." I set the fifty down on the bar and smoothed it out lovingly. "How's about you pour a whiskey for me, one for yourself, and I pay for the whole bottle? All nice and chummy. You like?"

"Chummy," he repeated, deadpan. "Isn't that what they feed to sharks? No thanks, Dalos. You're bad news, everyone knows it. Bad things happen to people who help you out."

I shot out both hands and dragged him halfway across the bar by the nonexistent lapels. The patrons in our immediate vicinity sized up unpleasantness in the making and made tracks. Nose to nose I told him, "Worse things happen to people who don't. Now you want to have a drink with your old buddy Tim or you want to spend the rest of your life in traction? Kind of hard to hold a brush when both your hands are broken, don't you think?"

He got someone to mind the bar and motioned for me to join him at a little table in the back. He had the brains to bring us a bottle of the good stuff. I watched him slam back three fast pick-me-ups before he asked, "So what do you want to know?"

"I want to see a man about a shoggoth," I said, and I told him all about Miss Whately's visit to my office. "I figure if anyone heard anything about that, it'd be you."

Pickman shook his head. "You figured wrong, Dalos. Soon as you said Vera Whately's name, I knew just how wrong. I'm your friend, so I'm going to give you a little free advice: Drop the case." He poured himself another shot and had the glass halfway to his mouth when I caught him by the throat and lifted him out of his chair. It was a waste of good whiskey, but I had a point to make.

"You're no one's friend, Pickman," I said, jerking him so close to my face that he could smell what I'd had for breakfast last Tuesday. "Not even your own. I'm not about to drop this case. The only thing I might consider dropping is you. Off the top of Coit Tower or the side of the Golden Gate; your choice."

"You wouldn't dare." His lips curled in a snarl.

"Yeah, I suppose you're right." I let go and he flopped back into his chair like a bundle of wetwash. "I guess I'm just an old softy. Couldn't hurt a fly. Love children and animals. Mostly animals." I gave him a slow, thin smile. "Mainly doggies. Ever met my doggies, Pickman?"

Pickman started to sweat. I guess he'd heard about my special pets, the Hounds. They're not exactly Westminster Kennel Club material, though they are pretty ... unique. You don't see dogs like the Hounds every day. Hell, you don't see them at all until it's too late. They're supernatural beasts that give pit bulls nightmares and make rabid Rottweilers look like Shirley Temple (The Good Ship Lollipop Years). I don't like to use the Hounds unless I've got to. Once I sic them on someone, they stay sicced. I can't call them off; no one can. They trail their quarry to the bitter, gruesome end in a way that puts bloodhounds and repo men to shame.

See, the Hounds have one teensy little advantage over other dogs: They can go through walls. Yeah, right through 'em, and I mean that literally, not like the way some overbred Golden Retriever goes charging headfirst into the plaster chasing an imaginary squirrel. Through the wall, no doggie door, no nothing. How do they do it? Damned if I know. It's what Sister Mary Azathoth used to call an Esoteric Mystery right before she smacked my knuckles with her ruler back in those carefree boyhood school days.

The Hounds can't use just any wall, though. They can only come at you through the angles of things, the sharp places where two planes intersect. You know the old joke "Run into the roundhouse, Nelly, he'll never corner you there"? Well, that's good advice if you're trying to dodge the Hounds.

I watched while Pickman glanced around his bar, nervous, counting the corners. All the Hounds need is one. I put two fingers to my mouth, like I was going to give 'em a whistle, took a deep breath, and then —

Pickman folded. Just the threat of the Hounds was enough to make him see reason. Five minutes later I walked out of his bar with a name, an address, and a blank bar tab. Good doggies.

I found what I was looking for in a dingy fleabag walk-up near Chinatown. Trouble was, someone else had found it before me. There wasn't enough left of that shoggoth to fill a wee-wee cup down at the Free Clinic. I looked around the ichor-splattered room. What a dump. It stank of stale beer, cheap patchouli incense and algae. Puddles of brackish water were everywhere, turning the late tenant's porno collection into a soggy mess.

Okay, into a soggier mess. I didn't know fish could do that sort of thing.

I chalked up my shoggoth hunt to the deadest of dead ends and figured I'd better get the hell out of there before the cops showed. Vera wasn't going to be happy: She'd specifically wanted that shoggoth delivered alive.

She'd just have to deal with disappointment: Things were tough all over, and they'd get tougher for me if I didn't beat it before the cops showed. I turned to go back to Pickman's on the slim-to-none chance he'd give me another lead, when someone snuck up behind me and kissed the back of my skull with a sock full of birdshot. I went down like a bathysphere.

By a remarkable coincidence, when I next opened my eyes I was in a bathysphere, or its ugly cousin. White, curved walls surrounded me. Like a luckless stand-up comedian, I couldn't find a straight line anywhere.

"Welcome back, Mr. Dalos."

The voice that filled the sphere was deep, rich and sweet as any chocolate from Ghiradelli Square. I packed on the pounds just listening to it. I sat up slowly, touched the back of my head just to make sure it was still attached, and tried to locate my host. Aside from the round, recessed lights, the only other architectural feature in my prison was one perfectly circular hatch. Whoever had laid me out in lavender must have used it to pop me into this joint like stuffing a pimento into an olive.

A round room. Round door. Round everything. I didn't need to have it spelled out in skywriting: My unknown warden knew enough about the Hounds to design a holding tank where I'd never be able to summon them to my rescue.

"Welcome yourself," I growled back. "Where are you?"

The sphere echoed with patronizing laughter. "I ask your indulgence in that matter, sir: Unlike a good child I am at my best when heard and not seen."

"You got a name to go with that snappy patter?" I asked. "Or should I just call you Noel Coward? The coward part fits."

That stung him. An edge crept into the voice: "Do not mistake discretion for cowardice, Mr. Dalos. If I conceal myself it is solely out of concern for your continued mental health. My physical aspect is one of such bizarre, grotesque monstrosity that the merest glimpse of my face is enough to turn strong men into babbling lunatics."

"So?" I shot back. "I used to date a Vassar girl. Bring it on."

"Hmmm. So did I. I see your point. Very well, Mr. Dalos, in that case — "

The walls went all eely, like a politician right before Election Day. Ripples of light formed themselves into a face that was part human, part batrachian, part octopoid, part icthyous, and part high school guidance counselor. Not the good parts. I couldn't help it: I covered my eyes and moaned.

"Ah! So you see for yourself how right I was to maintain my anonymity," the voice said. It sounded triumphant, but also a little ... sad.

It's tough when a man's been beat with the Ugly stick, but this guy had been marinated in Ugly juice, dipped in Ugly breadcrumbs, popped into the Ugly deep-fat fryer, slapped onto the Ugly plate with a side of Ugly slaw, garnished with the Ugly parsley, and –

Damn, I was hungry! I took a deep breath, opened my eyes, and lied like my ex-wife.

"Don't flatter yourself," I said. "I wasn't moaning about you, Handsome. I was just blackjacked, remember? It still hurts." I looked him right in the eyes when I said it. This was a tall order, considering their placement on his bulbous skull. Flounders had nothing on him.

"Oh." He looked sheepish. (Great, another animal to add to that one-man menagerie he had going on.) "My mistake. You are . . . a gracious man, Mr. Dalos."

"I'm a regular prince. Now let's use the correct fork to cut through all this bullshit: Tell me why you tried to have your own sister killed by a shoggoth . . . Mr. Whately!"

The vision of loveliness on the wall blanched. "How did you know my name?"

"Elementary, my dear — Oops, sorry: Wrong pastiche. What I mean is, with a kisser like yours, it doesn't take Einstein to figure it out. The Whatelys always had a thing for crossbreeding; everyone knows it. Your old New England sea captain ancestors married outside their faith, their race, their species and their galaxy. America's all about diversity, but you Whatelys were . . . overachievers. Not that there's anything wrong with that. Let me guess: Vera's your fully-human half-sister. Your daddy's a nameless horror from beyond the stars with a bad case of facial tentacles and a fondness for blondes, right?"

Whately looked puzzled. "My father is no nameless horror: His name is Vincent, like mine, and he's an orthodontist from Woonsockett, Rhode Island. Vera and I are fraternal twins." He sighed. "I'm just rat-butt ugly. That was why the Cousins' Club chose me for the sacrifice to the Great Old Ones during the big family reunion and clambake of ought-one."

He lapsed into a pretty damn sarcastic imitation of some of his relatives: "'Sure, let's toss 'em good old Vinnie: Who'll ever miss him? We'll please our deathless masters, hasten the day of the Elder Gods' return, advance the cause of bloody-minded chaos, and help keep America beautiful. Bonus!'" His lips curved into a sardonic grimace. "That was when Cousin Ira pantsed me and the rest of them threw me off the raft, into the icy depths of the sea."

It was my turn to look puzzled. "Vinnie — okay if I call you Vinnie? — I've got to say, you're looking pretty good for a guy who was sacrificed to the Great Old Ones."

When Vinnie laughed — even a short, bitter one like that — you could count his fillings. "Mr. Dalos — Tim — have you ever heard the phrase *too ugly to die?*"

"You mean — ?"

He shrugged his shoulders. (I think those were shoulders.) "Rejected. Rejected utterly. My family's sorcerous talents combined themselves with the powers of the Great Old Ones so that I might survive beneath the waves. Thus I was brought alive unto the awful fane of sunken R'lyeh, there to await my inevitable destruction. But nothing happened."

"R'lyeh . . . " I rubbed my chin. Sunken R'lyeh, a name to conjure with: R'lyeh, the lost city, the city beneath the waves; R'lyeh, where great C'thulhu lies dreaming, awaiting the day when his followers will bring about his return to obscene and terrible dominion; R'lyeh, where cyclopean architecture rules, massive walls tower at unthinkable angles, and you can't get a decent bagel to save your life. "A sacrifice rejected by C'thulhu? That's a first. I heard he'll eat anything."

"Sorry to disillusion you." Whately sounded miffed. "He said something about being on the South Beach diet. Oh, he was perfectly polite, for an unthinkable abomination; very Princetonian, in fact."

I tried to jolly up the poor sap: "How does it feel to be the one that got away?"

A funny look came into his eye (the top one). "But I didn't get away," he said.

"Though the nighted streets of sunken R'lyeh did not harbour my death, they proved to be an inescapable route to the utter captivity of my heart."

"Say what?"

"I met someone," he said, looking coy. (Or in his case, koi.) "Though my relatives intended me to bait Great C'thulhu's appalling appetites, I was the one who fell in love, hook, line and sinker. No pun intended, bien sûr."

I could see where this was going and decided to stop playing it cute before Whately applied his fondness for wordplay over to easy targets like bobber and rod. ("No pun intended" my bien sûr ass.)

"Nice going, Vinnie," I said. "Love, huh? Mutual, I hope?" He nodded. "Who's the lucky girl?"

He made a sound like a python trying to cough up a tapir and for a second I was afraid he was really choking on something. If he died, who'd spring me from my spherical cell? Then I realized he was simply pronouncing the name of his beloved.

"No," I said, shaking my head in denial. "You can't mean it. She isn't — "

"His daughter. Yes, she is. Great C'thulhu's child." He repeated her gagging-python name, then added: "But I call her Cupcake."

Cupcake. Great. Now I was going to shudder with nameless dread every time I walked past a bakery.

"Sweet little love story there, Vinnie: My heart's all melted and trickling down my pants' leg. What's any of it got to do with siccing a shoggoth on Vera?"

"It was a warning shoggoth," he protested. So Vera'd been right.

"A warning for what?"

"A warning that my greedy sister had better hand over the . . . item."

"The item?" I repeated.

"Yes, sir: The . . . item. The one that I . . . requested from her over six months ago." (Uh-oh. It's never good news when the other guy starts ladling on the Significant Pauses like that.) "A small obsidian image of the god Shub-Niggurath, also known as the Black Goat of the Woods with a Thousand Young. I asked for its loan most urgently after Cupcake and I returned from our elopement to Las Vegas. It is an indispensable part of the dark ritual that permits one of the Great Old Ones to assume mortal form."

"Why would you need — ?" I bit my tongue. I knew the answer before I finished the question.

Whately blushed, confirming my stomach-churning suspicions. "We — my bride and I — C'thulhu's daughter — my darling Cupcake, she — she takes after her father in a really big way. Size does not matter when Great C'thulhu mates with mortal women — my female ancestors did that a time or two in the past and none of the ladies involved ever seemed to mind. I read their journals: Page after page of praise to the Great Old One, interspersed with some very, er, graphic watercolours. However, when the honeymoon is on the other foot — "

"Say no more!" I cried. "Really. Don't. Look, I understand your problem. Your sister's my client, but I don't think I'll be letting her down if I play peacemaker for you two crazy kids. Let me out of here and I'll get her to hand over the image."

Whately wasn't buying. "Why should I trust you?"

"Come on, Vinnie, we're both men, right? Even if I don't understand what you see in your ... Cupcake, I sure as hell know all about wanting that sweet, sweet frosting. Got it?"

"Not yet." A slow smile made Whately look almost tolerably repulsive. "But with your help, I will."

I called Vera to let her know about the dead shoggoth. She wasn't happy. Then I told her all was not lost: I'd managed to pick up a good lead while casing the corpus deliquescent. It was true, in a way.

"So you've got a lead," she said. "Why aren't you following it?"

"Sister, do I tell you how to run your esoteric financial empire? Don't go telling me how to run my seedy, two-bit P.I. op." Yeah, I took a hard line with her. I wanted her angry. Angry people make mistakes. "This lead's gonna take me straight to the man who put you in the shoggoth crosshairs. Trust me, he's not the sort who'll come along quietly. You want in on the kill or not?"

"Why, Mr. Dalos, you sly dog!" I swear I could hear her licking her chops on the other end of the wires. "You certainly do know how to give a girl what she wants."

I grinned. The old Dalos charm was still working. "Listen, Vera," I said. "I've got another reason for this little invitation. There's something I need you to do for me. I'm packing enough heat to handle things if our little pal keeps it polite, but if he decides to go eldritch on us, we'll need some serious backup. What've you got in the arcane arsenal, dollface?"

She went through about a half-dozen assorted charms and talismans before she mentioned the image of Shub-Niggurath. "Bingo. Pop it in a plain brown wrapper and bring it along."

"Why that particular item?" she asked. "Some of the other objects I mentioned have far more power."

A guy could almost think she didn't trust me. "You like using a two-ton weight to squash a mouse, dollface?" I asked.

"As a matter of fact — "

"Because I don't like wasting anything, including sorcery. That image of old Shubya's perfect: Small enough for a concealed carry, just enough firepower to take down our target without attracting attention. Too big a boom and your stockholders will be reading all about it in tomorrow's papers. You want that?"

She didn't answer. The silence lasted a long time, so long that I thought she'd hung up on me for cracking wise. I was about to hang up myself when I heard her clear her throat and say, "You're right, of course, darling. I'll do whatever you say."

We agreed to meet in Chinatown, in the same sleazy hotel room where the shoggoth had bought a one-way ticket to Primal Goo Land. I told her to be there at 9, then told Vinnie to get there by 9:15 at the latest. No sense dragging this out. Either we'd have a happy family reunion, Vera all sorry for how she'd treated her brother, ready to hand over the image and give Vinnie his happy-ever-after with Cupcake, or else things would get real ugly real fast.

As for me, I went up to the room at 8 to make sure that there weren't going to be any surprises. None I hadn't planned, that is.

I opened the door, stepped inside, closed it after me quick and had my finger on the light switch when I heard: "Turn on the lights and you're a dead man, Dalos."

Even in the dark, I knew that voice: "Pickman!"

He was seated in a saggy armchair over by the window. The hotel's neon sign painted his face with brush strokes of bloody light and dirty shadow. I could just make out his shape, including the unmistakable outline of the .45 in his hand. It was something right out of an old Wild West pulp magazine, probably a prop from his studio, but if a coward like Pickman was toting it for self-protection, I'd bet it was in perfect, deadly working order.

"What the hell are you doing here?" I demanded. My fingers began to form the series of mystic signs that would silently summon the Hounds to my side. If he wanted to keep us both in the dark, maybe I could use it to my advantage.

Something bit my fingers so hard I screamed. A hand clamped itself across my mouth. Not a lot of ordinary hands feel or smell like a slab of calf's foot jelly, but I wanted to hold onto my sanity, so I decided I'd call it a hand 'til the cows came home.

"Ah, ah, ah, Dalos. A good dick is a quiet dick." Pickman was enjoying himself. "Why don't you settle down until our guests arrive? Maybe afterwards the two of us can grab a drink and maybe get you some iodine and a bandage for your fingers. Shoggoth bites can go to gangrene so easily."

"I'm sure Tim knows all about shoggoths, Mr. Pickman." A sweet, husky voice purred in my ear even as the gelatinous paw across my mouth tightened its grip. Vera! The tip of her tongue traced a light, tantalizing trail down my cheek. "He's not merely well-informed: He's that rarest of commodities, an honourable man. If he gives us his word that he'll keep quiet until this ... business with my brother is settled, we can trust him."

"I don't know, Vera." I saw Pickman shake his head slowly. "If we let him open his yap, what's to stop him from summoning those Hounds of his?"

Vera crossed the cramped, red-litten space between me and Pickman in two strides, gave the would-be artist a couple of swift belts to the chops, and was back at my shoggoth-saddled side in a heartbeat.

"First of all, you do not have the privilege of calling me by my first name," she said coldly. "Secondly, do you have any idea with whom you're dealing? I am a Whately! Long before the Hounds of Tim Dalos were paper-trained, my ancestors bargained away a share of their humanity for powers beyond your most demented dreams. If I say he'll stay silent until Vinnie gets here, he will, or his silence will be eternal." Vera's face floated in the darkness, suddenly glowing with its own weird, silvery light. I'm no creampuff, but the sight of that ghastly mask of naked ruthlessness dipped my heart in ice-water.

"Well, Tim?" she said, the wild white light fading to a softer glow. "Do we have your word of honour? Will you keep your mouth shut?"

I nodded. The paw across my mouth dropped and I sensed the shoggoth backing away from me. Vera smiled. "You don't have to be that quiet, darling," she said. "You just can't do anything to tip off my brother. And you can't summon the Hounds to attack us until Vinnie's taken care of."

"By the black basalt plinth of Great C'thulhu's most unholy altar, by the lurking madness, by the blood-thirst of the dhôles, and by T'sathoggua's most foul and unholy powers, you have my word," I said. "Pinky swear."

I kissed the tip of my little finger to seal that blasphemous bond, then added, "How long have you been onto my plan?"

"About luring me here for an undesired meeting with my brother? From the moment you became so insistent about my bringing one particular item to this rendezvous. That's when I dropped out of our conversation just long enough to put my own shoggoth to work. The creature is quite the skilled wiretapper. I knew you told my brother to be here by 9:15 as soon as he did. Very convenient, as it so happens: This whole nasty affair will end at 9:16 and I'll get home in time to catch the second half of CSI."

She folded her arms and looked thoughtful. "One thing still puzzles me, though: Vinnie's been after me to loan him the Black Goat for months. It's the first time he's ever shown any interest in such things. Why now?"

Before I could give her the capsule version of Vinnie's heart-warming little love story we heard footsteps in the corridor outside. I frowned. It was only 8 when I'd shown up and found Pickman already in place. Vera got there early, too. Vinnie wasn't supposed to arrive until after 9. Could a whole hour have passed? Sure, time flies when you're having fun, but fun and shoggoth fingers over my mouth while a demented doll like Vera Whately threatens my life aren't synonyms in any thesaurus I ever saw.

Vera and Pickman tensed like a pair of over-stretched rubber bands. The failed artist aimed his gat at the door, ready to blast the next person he saw to Kingdom-of-the-Great-Old-Ones-Come-Back. Vera's hand dipped into her pocketbook. I expected her to pull out her own gun, but instead of the glint of steel, I saw the glitter of obsidian.

It was the image of Shub-Niggurath. Vera's hand was shaking. Nerves. The same nerves that made her drop the glamour she'd been wearing all along. There's just so much coverup a doll can get from Max Factor. Suddenly I saw the family resemblance between her and Vinnie. She turned her head only slightly in my direction, managing to keep one eye on me, one on the door. (When your ancestors put in hard time mating with C'thulhu's

goggle-eyed kin, you get peripheral vision to burn.)

"Surprised?" she said. "Yes, I brought it. I want to see the look on Vinnie's face when he thinks he's about to realize his fondest dreams and then . . ." Her cruel smile stretched ear-to-ear.

"I don't get it, Vera," I said, keeping my voice low. The steps in the hall were getting closer, louder. "I know how these eldritch doodads work: Big or small, they've got bottomless reserves of sorcerous oomph, with a little arcane ah-ooh-gah to spare. It's not like your Shubby's gonna run out of juice if Vinnie borrows it. Hell, he'd probably even pay you for it! So why not play nice? He's your brother. Blood is thicker than water."

"Mmmmm, yes, it is." Vera licked her lips. "You're a very persuasive man. Under other circumstances, I might allow you to convince me to help my brother. There's just one thing holding me back: I hate him. All the Whatelys do. He's abominable, even by our standards. The list, scope and magnitude of his offenses is so great that he was cast out of the family years ago. Why do you think I am the sole heir to the Hezekiah Whately shipping empire? And if you say 'Because you look like a sole,' I will smack you silly."

Damn, she was a sharp cookie. I bit my tongue, then took a deep breath and said, "It's kind of hard to imagine something nasty enough to get the Whately family panties in a bunch. You want to give me a for-instance?"

Vera's expression hardened. "He's a traitor to his kind: A renegade, an apostate. He doesn't believe in the return of the Great Old Ones, he's never sacrificed so much as a telemarketer to C'thulhu, and he hasn't attended a single Cousins' Club meeting in over twenty years!"

"But if that's true — "

I didn't get the chance to finish. The door opened. A misshapen silhouette stood backlit in the archway. Vera held out the image of the Black Goat like a really stupid kid taunting a Doberman with a bratwurst.

"Come and get it!" Vera crowed just before Pickman pulled the trigger.

A shot rang out. A body hit the floor. The shoggoth screamed and my whole world turned into an avalanche of angry mackerel. Wave after wave of fish flooded the cheesy hotel room. I was knocked off my feet and pulled beneath the surface in an undertow of fins, scales and stink. Somewhere I heard Pickman gargling baby jellyfish while he fired off round after round into the bouillabaise of doom engulfing us all.

Then it got silent.

I flailed my way out from under the perch and pollock, breaking the surface and gasping for air. The room was still dark, the crimson light of the neon sign outside now glittering over a scaly sea. I tried to stand upright, but it was too slimy underfoot to keep my balance. I was about to slip back beneath the fetid surface when a strong hand reached out, hooked me by the back of my jacket, and dragged me to the safety of the hall.

All right, so it wasn't exactly a hand.

"Yo. How you doin'?" The shoggoth brushed stray scales off my lapels.

"I'm okay," I said. "I think." I looked down. A monstrous,

titanic body slumped on the linoleum, blocking most of the hall-way. A single tentacle trailed across the slowly spreading pool of ichor, its silver charm bracelet catching the light from the naked bulb overhead. I sucked in my breath. I'd never seen her before in my life — unless you count nightmares — but I knew who she was. No one could fill out an angora sweater quite like Great C'thulhu's little girl. This was bad.

"Cupcake," I breathed.

"Yeah, I could eat somethin'," the shoggoth said. Then it noticed what I was talking about. "Oh. Wow. The boss' daughter. We're in deep silt now."

I cast a quick glance back into the hotel room. Somewhere under that pile-up of sushi-to-go lay Vera Whately and Pickman. If they weren't dead, they would be. If they were lucky.

I summoned the Hounds.

Three minutes and some very specific instructions later all the fish were gone, I'd saved a bundle on dogfood, and the shog-goth and I were staring down at Vera's corpse. Pickman was nowhere to be seen. Either the Hounds had gotten careless during their mop-up operation or that quick-on-the-trigger bastard had managed to tunnel his way through Flounder Mountain and duck out the window.

"Guess I better call the boys in blue," I said. I looked at Cupcake's body. "What a heartbreak. Poor Vinnie. He's going to show up at nine and find this."

"Nah," said the shoggoth. "Movie don't get out 'til eleven."

"What did you say?"

"Hey, last I saw him, he was going to the movies, seven o'clock show at some artsy-fartsy place down in the Castro. Double feature, two scoops of celluloid crap for the price of one, you dig?"

I gritted my teeth. "I dig."

I dug too much, too late, but I dug.

I hunkered down beside Vera's body and pried the small obsidian image of Shub-Niggurath out of her cold, clenched, dead hand.

It was almost midnight when I found Vinnie propping up the bar in a Mission District dive. He was sucking down Martinis, his ugly mug warped by a smug smile.

"Hello, Vinnie." I slipped onto the stool next to him. "Missed you at the party."

Vinnie froze at the sound of my voice, then his hand dove inside his jacket.

The other boozehounds thought they knew what that move meant. They scattered like paranoid chipmunks.

I was the only one who knew he wasn't going for a gun.

The wand was black and silver, the tip a tiny ivory skull with rinky-dink bat-wings sticking out at the sides. Arcane kitsch you could pick up at any sci-fi convention, only this one had the power of a genuine wizard behind it. It glowed like Christmas.

"So you caught wise, Mr. Dalos," he rumbled.

"What, I'm 'Mr. Dalos' again? What happened to 'Tim'? I thought we were pals, Vinnie. I thought I was the answer to your bachelor prayer."

"So you were; just not the one you anticipated." Vinnie's pompous chuckle was only half as attractive as his face. The

wand crackled, surrounding him in a bubble of purple light. "She's dead, isn't she?"

"Which 'she,' Vinnie? Your sister or your wife?"

"Judging by that look of human compassion you can't quite manage to suppress, I'd say the answer must be both."

It took every ounce of self-control to keep me from going for my gun and blasting his arrogant grin all the way to Innsmouth. I held back. I knew that if I tried anything noble (read: stupid) he'd pulverize me. A heroic (read: really stupid) death would have to wait. I couldn't die just yet: Unfinished business.

"You never loved her, did you?" I said. "Cupcake, I mean. You went after her because you knew you could use her, and that's exactly what you did. Poor kid. It must've been lonely, being C'thulu's daughter. Lonely enough for her to go ga-ga over the first man to pay attention to her, even if he was a piece of dirt like you. You set her up, sending her to the hotel like that. Did you know Pickman would be there? That he'd panic and start shooting up the joint?"

Vinnie shrugged. "I didn't bank on it. I'm not fool enough to leave such important matters to chance. My own informants told me my sister had enlisted his aid, I knew the man's lack of nerve, but he was never key to my master plan."

"Which was to kill Vera," I said.

Vinnie beamed smarmy approval at me for being so damn clever. "I told Cupcake to bring back the image of Shub-Niggurath. I knew Vera would never give it to her any more than she'd give it to me. That would make dear Cupcake so angry. She is — was — a most determined female. A fight to the death was inevitable. If Cupcake perished in that encounter, I knew that the death-throes of a Great Old One's spawn would destroy Vera as well. And if Cupcake killed Vera but survived ... Well, I'd live with that. Politics isn't the only thing that makes strange bedfellows."

"Only now you get to play the grieving widower," I sneered. "You never loved her at all, did you? Poor Cupcake. If she'd lived, how long before you would've gotten rid of her?"

"Oh, I'd never have done that, sir." He helped himself to a handful of peanuts from the bowl in front of him. "That would be suicidal. Kill one of C'thulu's spawn, die in the backwash, that's the rule."

"Vera said you didn't believe in the Great Old Ones."

"I didn't believe in serving them. I do believe in letting them serve me. Imagine my surprise when I discovered that they actu-ally exist! But I could have employed them to my own ends even if they'd been mere figments of the imagination. There's nothing easier than using another person's faith as your cat's-paw."

"You're scum, Whately," I said, and spat in his eye. The glob hit the bubble of protective sorcery surrounding him and sizzled away to a wisp of steam.

He shrugged. "I am merely the engineer of my own destiny. The Great Old Ones have given me the golden key to my late sis-ter's fortune. She was too cocky to bother making a will. I am her only possible heir. And now that my wife has gone to that big catfood factory in the sky, Vera's money will buy me the com-panionship of more . . . comely females."

"You set her up. You set us all up. You knew which buttons to push and your stubby little fingers gave them the full Van Cliburn treatment."

"Careful, sir: You'll have an apoplexy if you don't master that self-righteous rage. What a pity that there's nothing you can do about it." Vinnie oozed complacency and assorted colloids.

I glared at him, but it was hard on the eyes. Eventually I let my shoulders slump. "Damn," I muttered. I leaned over the bar, snagged me a bottle of Old Batrachian, and took a swig straight from the neck.

Vinnie smirked. "Is that how you hard-boiled, er, dicks concede defeat? By going on a bender?"

I shrugged and took another hit of booze. "Is that how you chum-suckers celebrate victory?" I countered. "By hogging the free peanuts?"

"Be my guest, sir; be my guest." He shoved the bowl in my direction. I fingered the goods thoroughly, grabbed a fistful, and shoved it back. The protective bubble surrounding him didn't interfere with his ability to gobble the rest of the nuts like they were going out of style. He just about licked the bowl clean.

"Take it easy, Porky," I said. "It'd be a shame if you choked."

His laugh bathed my face in hot gusts of peanutty rudeness. "Would you be so very sorry to see me die?" he asked archly.

"No," I replied. "Only that I won't be able to watch it happen." I turned my back on Vinnie and strode out of the bar, muttering one last word under my breath as I left.

The shoggoth was waiting for me out on the street. It opened its mouth to speak, but that was when the screams started.

"Holy T'sathouggua on a cracker, what in hell is that?" the shoggoth demanded.

"That is Vinnie Whateley being forcibly reunited with his late wife and sister," I said, brushing one finger smartly along the brim of my fedora. "Eventually."

"Huh? Come on, word on the abysmally nighted street says he's a top-notch wizard. You telling me he didn't have a protective spell up?"

"Oh, he did. Real pretty, top of the line. Nothing got in or out without his say-so." I flashed the shoggoth a grin. "Did I ever tell you about what good hunting dogs the Hounds are? I want them to annihilate one blade of grass in a field of millions, it's gone. One grain of wheat in a packed silo? It's history. One — "

"Yeah, but if the man they're after's got a shielding spell — " the shoggoth protested.

"Now who said I sicced them on a man?" I asked, all innocent. One last unearthly shriek from inside the bar shattered the night like a four-year-old with a mallet and a kewpie doll. In the damp, pungent silence that followed, I added: "Just a peanut." I winked at the shoggoth. "Funny thing about shielding spells: They only protect a man from the outside. You'd be surprised how many angles there are inside the human body, or how many places the chomped-up bits of one little peanut can go. But that won't — didn't — stop the Hounds. They always get exactly what I send them after, down to the very last crumb. Anything else ... well, that's what we in the trade like to call collateral damage."

I strolled back to the door of the bar and glanced inside. "Must've been something he ate," I remarked. The shoggoth made the mistake of sneaking a peek over my shoulder. It was still puking its guts out in the gutter as I walked past it and head-ed back to my office.

He was waiting for me when I got there. Amazing how he wedged his rubbery bulk into the client's chair. I made a big deal out of taking off my jacket nice and slow, then hanging it neatly. I forced myself to act as if finding him in my office was no big deal. The truth was, when I saw those obsidian eyes, that squamous skin, those tentacles, talons, and tailored suit, I felt my insides turn to oatmeal. With raisins.

I squeezed past him and sat behind my desk. "Well, this is an unexpected privilege," I said, opening the bottom file drawer and taking out the whiskey bottle and a pair of grimy shot glasses. "To what do I owe the honour?"

The dread Elder God looked at me with ichor-shot eyes. "I came here to thank you, Mr. Dalos," he said. At least that's what I think he said. He had a pretty thick R'lyehvian accent.

"What for?" I asked. But I knew.

C'thulhu's bat wings rustled as he shifted in the chair. "I tried to warn her," he said. "I tried to tell her that Vinnie Whately was no good, but she wouldn't listen. They never do, when they're in love. Have you ever raised a daughter, Mr. Dalos?"

"None of my own. But they say that the first twenty thousand years are the hardest."

Great C'thulhu sighed. "I couldn't stop her and I couldn't save her. At least you were able to avenge her. That's why I came here, to thank you for that."

"Don't mention it. Vinnie Whately was garbage. What I did was a public service, helping keep our fair city clean. Anyway, the Hounds did all the real work. Tell you what, buy 'em a couple boxes of dog biscuits and we'll call it square."

The lord of sunken R'lyeh gave me a look of grudging admiration. "Of course, Mr. Dalos. In addition, the next time you check your savings account, you'll find a little something extra in it: Just a modest gift from anonymous 'friend.' Use it well. Buy new chairs."

I grinned. "You know, sir, for someone who spends most of his time dreaming away the ages until your followers can help you destroy the world of men and establish a kingdom of cosmic chaos, madness, and delirium, you're okay."

I poured two shots of rye and shoved one in his direction. Everything had come full circle. The case that began with Vera Whately wanting payback for her shoggoth bite had ended with me avenging that and more. All nice and neat. So why did I feel like such a mess on the inside?

I raised my glass. I never expected to find myself sharing a snort of rotgut with a being from beyond the stars. What's the proper toast to offer an Elder God? Here's mud in your obsidian eye? Down the tentacled hatch? L'chayim?

What the hell; I improvised:

"Here's looking at you, squid."

And that really was the beginning of a beautiful friendship. ⏎

Nebula Award winner Esther Friesner is the author of 31 novels and over 150 short stories, in addition to being the editor of seven popular anthologies. Her latest publications include Nobody's Princess, Temping Fate, *and* Death and the Librarian and Other Stories. *She is married, the moth-*

ILLUSTRATION BY KRYSTIAN POLAK

IT'S THE END OF THE WORLD
AS WE KNOW IT, AND
I FEEL ...?

The View
From Here

by Morgan Llywelyn

I t is terribly cold here at the end of the world. The wind that rises from the abyss shrieks like a soul in torment. In spite of that howling wind I occasionally summon enough courage to creep to the edge and peer down. It is still not possible to believe what I see — or rather, what I do not see.

For I see nothing.

Nothing. My straining, watering eyes behold no terrestrial object, no distant sun, no star, not even the blackness of space itself.

Nothing.

How can you see nothing? That was, I believe, a question posed to Alice by one of the queens. I'm not sure which one; my memory has gone askew. If any copy of *Alice in Wonderland* still existed I could look it up. When I first read those words they seemed, paradoxically, both logical and nonsensical. They still do. Yet that is what my eyes report when I gaze into the void. Literal, absolute, nothing.

In "The Colour Out of Space," H. P. Lovecraft posited the existence of a color no one had ever seen before. Reading that story as a teenager, I was struck by the brilliance of his concept, which stretched human imagination beyond its bounds. Now a terrible reality has gone one step farther. Even Lovecraft did not dare to imagine the Nothing which is all I have left.

It began so simply; just a little thing. Watching television one evening I was mildly disturbed by a program which listed the species, both plant and animal, that had disappeared from the planet in the last decade. The number was appalling in its sheer volume. I watched, shook my head, clucked my tongue, made an appropriate comment to my wife, then put the subject out of my mind.

A few nights later there was a documentary on the growing holes in the ozone layer, but I did not connect it with the earlier program on extinctions. In fact, several months passed before I began to make conscious note of the number of news reports concerning disappearance per se. Throughout history people have disappeared, of course; Judge Crater and Lord Lucan were hardly unique. But now broadcasters were puzzling over the vanishing of one well-known individual after another, from rock stars to nuclear scientists to politicians. No great loss, any of them, I thought to myself. Until I realised that ordinary people were being reported as missing, too. Hundreds of them. And then thousands.

Trying not to sound as anxious as I felt, I urged my wife Virginia to carry her cell phone with her at all times, even when she went out into the garden. She pooh-poohed me, but at least she did as I asked. When I telephoned our children — Bob in the military and Laura in college — their responses were typical of their generation. I should have more faith in them, they could take care of themselves. And besides, there really was nothing to worry about.

They were right, of course. I was being over-sensitive and over-protective, two charges that frequently have been levelled at me over the years. I have attempted to suppress these tendencies. My profession, that of an accountant, actively discourages the use of the imagination. My life has been spent in the quiet backwaters. Reading, stamp collecting, helping my wife in the garden — these have been my gentle pastimes. If men of my age still wore suspenders I would have been a belt-and-suspenders man.

I began reading the newspapers more thoroughly, collecting random bits of information. Nothing made the television unless it was considered a major event, but newspapers are a wonderful source of small items that few people ever notice. Except I was noticing them, now. Seeing them as part of a jigsaw I had no idea how to put together.

Something had definitely gone wrong with the world. Aided and abetted by their governments, big corporations were stripping away the planet's natural resources with increasing abandon. The results in terms of damage to the environment were becoming increasingly obvious, but nobody stopped it. The environmentalists staged protest marches and lobbied the politicians relentlessly, but they could not compete with the lure of profit. It seemed nothing could compete with the lure of profit. We had enough yet we wanted more. We humans always wanted More.

The result, with a terrible balancing of the cosmic scales, would be Less.

One Saturday morning, when I went out to replenish the numerous bird feeders we kept around the garden, I discovered that they were still full. I asked Virginia if she had refilled them recently but she denied it, reminding me that this was one of my jobs. My every-Saturday-morning jobs. She did remark, however, that there had been a singular absence of birdsong lately.

Ignoring the disquiet gnawing my belly, I tried to offer a

rational explanation. "It's the heavy machinery on the new highway they're building," I said. "The noise is probably scaring off the birds."

"That construction is over a mile away," Virginia replied with a frown. "We can't even hear it from here, so I don't see how it could possibly be frightening our birds."

"Their hearing is more sensitive than ours. And they pick up vibrations," I said as if I knew.

The late newscast that night reported that nothing had been heard from our weather stations and military posts north of the Arctic Circle since Thursday afternoon. The newscaster tried to sound calm. Before the program was over he announced that other countries with outposts in that region had not heard from their bases, either. This time he seemed more sombre.

By Sunday morning, national governments were accusing one another of dire but unnamed actions. Threats and sabre rattling choked the electronic airwaves. War was the only answer. Nations on both sides of the globe began preparing for conflict, even as search parties hurried to the locales of supposed disaster and . . . did not return.

On Monday new expeditions were sent out but contact was lost with them almost at once. A frightening silence lay over the far north and began extending southward. All transmission from Victoria Island and Point Barrow ceased. Simultaneously a silence more profound than that of glaciers descended over the Antarctic. It too began expanding outward. Northward.

Hysteria set in. By Tuesday our government, all governments, were giving out frantic and contradictory messages, blaming one another while attempting to reassure their own populace. Military preparations stepped up alarmingly throughout Wednesday and Thursday morning.

That afternoon I telephoned my son again. Bob was stationed in Presque Isle, Maine, so I called from my office rather than running up the phone bill at home. Besides, I didn't want Virginia to overhear and become more upset than she already was. Bob had just told me that the Air Force was ordering another recon flight to Baffin Bay when the phone went dead. At first I thought the connection had been broken, but when I asked the operator to reconnect us she told me there was no response.

"None at all?"

"No, sir. In fact, I suppose I shouldn't be telling you this, but we haven't been able to put through any phone calls to Canada for the last half hour. I don't know what's happening but I think I'm going to go home now. My boss can just take this job and . . ."

I found myself listening to dead air. For a couple of seconds I stood holding the receiver in my hand, staring at it. Then I dropped the instrument and ran to get my coat and hat. I was going home, too.

Word was already out. Though it was not yet rush hour, the streets of the city were thronged with people frantically trying to go someplace. I hurried to the parking lot where I kept my car, only to find it was impossible to get it out. The street in front was jammed solid with cars. Anxious drivers were shouting at one another and honking their horns, creating a cacophony like the orchestration of doom.

Across the street from the parking lot was a bicycle shop. In the past I often had gazed in the window, musing over memories of boyhood joys. I ran to the shop and was relieved to find the owner still there. Opening my wallet, I took out every bill I had and thrust them into his hands. "A bicycle, any bicycle!"

He grinned at me. "Sure, fella. Looks like this might be my lucky day, you're the third person in here in the last five minutes."

"I'm sure you'll sell a hundred more in the next ten minutes," I told him.

With a bike I was able to weave my way through stalled traffic while frustrated drivers glared at me. As I rode I used my mobile phone to try to reach Virginia, but there was a lot of interference and the signal kept breaking up. When I got home she was waiting for me on the front porch. She threw her arms around me in an uncharacteristic public display of affection. "Thank God you're here! I was just about to drive my car into town and try to find you."

"I'm glad you didn't, the city's in chaos. I'm going to stay right here now, because until we know what's going on we mustn't get separated. Do we have enough supplies to last until . . . well, for a while, anyway?"

"When I went to the supermarket yesterday afternoon," she said, "they hadn't restocked, though they usually do it on Wednesday morning. The shelves were practically empty. I couldn't get half the things on my list. We're almost out of toilet paper!" she added with a shaky little laugh, as if that were the worst possible catastrophe.

I hurried to turn on the television and get the cable news. Reports were flooding in from all over the globe, so fast the commentators could not keep up with them. Then all at once, it stopped. Just stopped. The rapidly spreading silence halted as abruptly as if it had run into a stone wall. No one could reach past that wall but at least it was no longer advancing. Everything on this side of it remained untouched and unharmed.

The world reeled, took a deep breath. Tried to figure out what happened. I left the TV on while an endless procession of scientists and experts speculated and prognosticated, and Virginia opened a can of spaghetti. We ate it cold, sitting in front of the set. Neither of us had any appetite. In the wee small hours of the morning it was officially confirmed that the plague, or

whatever it was, had indeed halted.

"Will things go back to normal now?" my wife asked. Her voice was shaking a little.

"I'm sure they will," I told her soothingly, though I was not at all sure. "There's a logical explanation for all this, you'll see; something to do with science."

"That's all right then," she said. "As long as it's not something to do with God."

We tumbled into bed and fell into an exhausted sleep, holding one another.

When we awoke in the morning things were, tentatively, beginning to return to normal. Although no one as yet had penetrated that strange silence and returned to tell the tale, business and industry were resuming. The great engines that ran the world as we knew it could not be stilled for long. I heard a thud as the paperboy threw our morning newspaper onto the porch, and when I switched on the television I was greeted by a commercial for a new model automobile. "More leg room and higher performance!" a voice announced triumphantly. "Your neighbours will be envious!" The world waited for an explanation of recent events. There was still talk of war but it was cautious talk, because no one knew just whom to attack or exactly why. But oil fields all around the globe were ordered to step up production drastically, while the munitions firms went into high gear. I insisted on accompanying Virginia when she went to the supermarket. Fortunately restocking had taken place. We returned laden with everything she could think of, including six months' supply of toilet paper. My wife had always been an avid consumer — one reason I was careful about pinching pennies — but even for her, it was an excessive shopping trip. She was not the only one, however. Shaken by recent events, the whole nation went on a shopping spree. "They're buying as if there's no tomorrow," a commentator remarked on TV. Tomorrow did come, of course. With a vengeance. I woke up alone. Lying not in my familiar bed, but on a bare patch of earth. No grass, no shrub, no tree. No birdsong. No Virginia. Thinking I was having a nightmare, I struggled to wake up. It was no nightmare. This altered reality went on and on like the watch I was still wearing, ticking away the minutes and hours as I sat on the ground in my pajamas, terrified. When my legs began to cramp I had to get up. One foot at a time, literally, I began exploring my surroundings. The bare earth extended for about a quarter of a mile in every direction. There were no paths, no roads, no houses. No trees or shrubs. Then abruptly even the earth itself came to an end. In the days when the world was familiar I used to enjoy science fiction. I recall one television program in which a suburban neighborhood was snatched away and transported to an alien planet, where the inhabitants were imprisoned within a shimmering force field. There was no force field here, though I would almost have welcomed one. I would have welcomed anything. Any thing. Instead there was nothing. Except that terrible howling wind, and you cannot see the wind. With considerable trepidation I thrust my hand forward. It did not disappear, I could still see my fingers in front of me in that awful emptiness. However the cold I felt against my skin was so intense I could not bear it for more than a few seconds. I snatched my hand back and warmed it in my armpit. If there had been something to hold onto, I might have leaned forward and looked down. But there was no tree I could grasp, no branch, no nice safety railing. Taking a deep breath to steady myself, I lay down on my belly at the very edge of . . . whatever it was . . . and peered down. A ghastly bout of vertigo left me deeply shaken. With my eyes tightly shut I inched my way backward, still on my belly, until I was several feet from the edge. Then I lay there and waited for my heart to stop pounding. At last I was able to raise myself on my hands and knees and crawl away. That was, I think, several days ago. Since then I have gone through a number of stages. The panic of a trapped rat, the terror of a frightened child, the despair of a dying man. There is nothing to eat and no water to drink. My situation has robbed me of normal hunger, though I am tormented by thirst. I trust it will not last long and I will soon die. I hope; I pray.

The alternative is too terrible to contemplate. Alas, there is nothing with which I could commit suicide. Can you see Nothing, Alice? I can. ⟲

Morgan Llywelyn was born in America of Irish parents. She published her first novel in 1978. She returned to Ireland permanently in 1985 and lives north of Dublin. She has published thirteen mainstream historical novels, including the international best seller Lion of Ireland *and the first three volumes of her Irish Century series.*

Her work also includes a non-fiction biography of Xerxes of Persia, *a number of short stories, and several books for children.*

Llwelyn is also the official Bard of Clan O'Brien and an honorary member of Clan Kavanagh.

The Other Wife

An Invocation to the Goddess Kali

BY ARRIN DEMBO

O Lord, come dance with me
in the light of the burning city.
Oh Father, pass your hand over my skin
blackened by the choking ash of the pyre.
Beloved, there is no turning back:
Our bridges are all afire.
Behold the wise come to bow before me,
to sip the wine from my cup,
to entwine my wrists and ankles
with living flesh.
I dwell upon the cosmic mountain.
I am the darkness
The terror
The wearer of skulls.
I am the formidable
The frightening
The frenzied
Feminine fire.
Behold the mouth which speaks only
truth
dripping with the gore of demons.
I am delight and daurmanasya:
Dangerous
Deadly
Drunk
Dancing…

Let me lick the blood from your beard,
Beloved.
Weave for me a garland
of fallen flowers.
Give to me the heads of sages
The arms of soldiers
The tongues of poets
The thighs of dancers
The eyes of painters
The loins of sinners
The heart of a saint.
I have come from the field of battle
glutted with the blood of my enemies.
The legions of the mad and mighty
the wicked and the wise
Prophets and princes
follow in my wake.
Lie with me in the cremation ground
in the dust of the dead.
Clutch the double moon
in your terrible hands.
Lie down in mirtasana;
I will ride the Pillar of Creation.
Spread your arms
like the crucified Christ.
Bellow your pleasure
Howl your pain.

I will resurrect you
again and again…
Kiss the lips of my three faces.
Kiss the lids of my three eyes.
Drink the milk, the blood, the ashes
from my laughing mouth.
Entangle yourself in the net
of my terrible deceptions--
the ragged tresses
as dark as death.
Soothe me with sacrifices
and the music of war:
With the tears of widows
With the wails of orphans
The song of jackals
The laughter of crows
The roar of cannons
The breaking of bones.
Adorn me with offerings
Smeared with the nectar of red red
blooms
with the glistening pearls
of your desire.
I will teach you the steps of the tandava
dance.
I am your other wife.
And my time is now. ⟲

Still More Demons

(OUT OF THE ALMOST 100 CONJURED VIA PEN AND RANDOM-NAME GENERATOR)

by Ben Towle

DANTALL

ERINA

ERISTOS

FENEX

FLAGARD

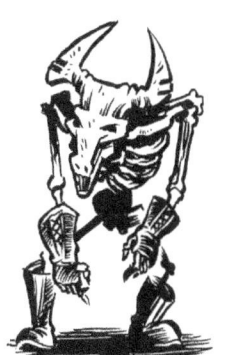

FOMODEUS

FORGOR

FURSUK

GARCHISI

resorting to spilled blood. *Miriam*, by Truman Capote, is a prime example of urban horror artfully realized. Capote was a mainstream writer, albeit one whose early work was often characterized by undertones of the supernatural, that strain of Gothic sensibility so typical in the work of many Southern writers. The source of horror in this story is nothing more apparently dangerous than a mysterious little girl whose visits to a middle-aged widow living alone in a Manhattan brownstone become gradually more ominous as some unstated element of malevolence is subtly suggested. The sense of horror is all the more effective for being understated and undefined, for developing as quietly as an approach of twilight.

Another story that profits by the same technique is Charlotte Perkins Gilman's *The Yellow Wallpaper*. In this late-nineteenth-century story a young woman, diagnosed with a nervous condition, becomes fixated on the yellow wallpaper in the nursery room of the house she and her husband have rented. The story describes the evolution of her insanity with chilling deliberation and virtuoso skill as she hallucinates menacing shapes and presences in the wallpaper. The story is pure mood and no other color could have been used so effectively as yellow, with its ominous associations — the color of arsenic, decay, candlelight, malady, the eyes of infernal creatures (Rosemary's baby!), waning sunlight. As for the latter, a poem by Emily Dickinson captures the mood achieved in *The Yellow Wallpaper* as effectively in just a few words:

> There's a certain Slant of light,
> Winter afternoons —
> That oppresses, like the Heft
> Of Cathedral tunes —
> When it comes, the Landscape listens
> Shadows — hold their breath —
> When it goes, 'tis like the Distance
> On the look of Death.

Another of my favorite short stories, arguably a horror story (although not urban horror), is Evelyn Waugh's "The Man Who Liked Dickens," which develops its mood even more subtly than the afore-mentioned two. The protagonist, the sole survivor of an ill-fated expedition in the remote Brazilian jungle, is found and nursed back to health by a white man living among Indians in an isolated location like Kurtz's in *Heart of Darkness*. The protagonist's host has a huge library of books but can't read, and during his convalescence the protagonist spends hours reading to his host. The former is eager to get back to civilization and the latter keeps putting him off, assuring him that before long a boat will arrive, but as weeks pass it becomes apparent that he will never get out of there because the host would then find himself alone again, shut out of the world of the imagination that books have opened to him.

All three of these stories build mood as quietly as a gathering of dark clouds on a summer day. And there is not a death in any of them. Not a drop of blood spilled. Each of these stories demonstrates that death is not the sole thematic province of the horror story. Loneliness, isolation, and madness are also eminently horrific.

Let's take a look at Michael Shea, one of the best contemporary horror-fiction writers and one whose work shows the strong influence of H.P. Lovecraft. Urban horror is rarely realized with more sophistication than in stories like "The Angel of Death," "Fat Face," and "The Horror on the #33." Here is a writer whose work is both visceral and cerebral. As I wrote in an introduction to Shea's book *I, Said the Fly:* "His prose is elegant and tough, intellectual and street-wise, it soars on updrafts of eloquence and swoops to drop napalm on the reader."

Of the aforementioned three stories, the first two have a temperament that is downright nasty, the third is somewhat serio-comic and reminiscent of Kafka. While these are all masterful, Shea's salient masterpiece is "The Autopsy," a science-fiction horror-story similar to *Alien* and also a story that illustrates how art can redeem material that might be objectionable if it were proffered merely for cheap thrills (like the slasher movies). In a literature course I once took, which was taught by Wright Morris, I remember him expressing disdain for modern writers who undertake to shock the reader without providing revelation.

"The Autopsy" is the flip side of urban horror, being set in a small town (Shea's versatility with settings is further demonstrated by "Uncle Tuggs," set in the backwoods of Northern California.) Shea draws on his experience from having lived in both metropolitan and rural areas, but "The Autopsy" can be cited as a model for aspiring writers for its conscientious application of research regarding a matter not part of his experience, namely the performance of an autopsy. The first-rate writer knows that there is no substitute for verisimilitude, and the verisimilitude in "The Autopsy" can be certified by the fact that the author received a number of complimentary letters from morticians.

Horror fiction is not fundamentally a literature of ideas, but a craftsman like Michael Shea will bring ideas to the market-place along with elegantly crafted prose. Of course ideas are implicit in the prose of a serious writer just as four-leaf clovers inhabit a field or veins of gold are found in bedrock.

I hesitate to even speculate about a prognosis for the commercial health of horror fiction, urban or otherwise, in the near future. The function of such fiction is to involve us vicariously in dangerous experiences, but if the reality of danger in our lives becomes commonplace it seems possible that the appeal of such fiction will diminish. Or is it so? One wonders how popular war movies are in Israel. In the meantime, the six o'clock news, always replete with horror, is enduringly popular. As the Jewish comedian said, "Go figure." 𝄞

As Larry Tritten puts it, 'I'm a veteran freelance writer (Scriptor horribilis) who has sold more than a thousand pieces since I came to San Francisco from the backwoods of northern Idaho, where I grew up in a mom-&-pop tavern (our customers were mostly loggers and miners). Spent three years in the Army Security Agency with a Top-Secret & Crypto clearance, in those days snooping on Red Chinese broadcasts. I never dreamed that forty years later I would be traveling in China on a press trip and be received with warm hospitality. Sold the first story I sent in at age 21 and it was the equivalent of being a vampire — I became one. I've been published in most of the genre magazines, metropolitan newspapers, and The New Yorker, and many other magazines."

Scars

by Leah Bobet

The night I delivered Chelsea's birthday gift, I found her smiling gloriously in a pool of her own blood.

Paper and lipsticks scattered everywhere as I searched a packed purse for my cellphone, stabbed at the small green numbers. By the time I picked them up again they were ruined, the cases stained just a shade off of the #284 Fire Engine Red of the ambulance lights. Although they jostled her on the gurney, poked her with needles and wrapped her in gauze, the grin never left Chelsea's face. I stood in the doorway an hour after they took her, still staring at the neat pile of her skin, at the hints of gray-green eyeshadow and dusky blush on the soggy shreds.

Even in the hospital, as the horrific cuts slowly healed, her disfigured face looked beatific — almost radiant. I sat beside her bed for months and watched the wounds heal into scars which drew down her glowing eyes.

She didn't speak to me much, but that was Chelsea's way. It took a week of asking before she admitted to the act, two of begging before she described how she took a paring knife to her own body and peeled it like an apple, round and round and raw.

When she transferred into the psych ward, the doctors were puzzled: no sign of depression. It took a month of pleading before she confessed that she had not wanted to die.

I started putting on a full face of makeup in the mornings.

I saw less of Chelsea when she left the hospital, covered in the red, dark, raised marks that caged her once swinging stride. I was one of the few former friends to brave her brand new, icy cold apartment, her shiny and smooth slashed face. She sat, cheerful in her sweatless body as I shivered in my coat, her speech slow and slurred. She seemed indifferent to the stares of both companions and strangers, only angered when I suggested surgery to restore her former beauty.

That was the one time she threw me out, swearing in her thickened, halting voice. That night, the shiny, smooth skin of her scars haunted my dreams. I spent hours imagining what it would be like to touch, to caress, to live inside.

All the while, something grew tight and uncomfortable inside me. I was used to the red welts on her face; the knotted tissue of her arms and chest I found oddly fascinating. Of all things, her triumph disgusted me. She had barely survived, then frightened and disowned everyone. I didn't know why she kept me around. We had history.

Sympathetic or not, I reached my limits. One night I started to scream, berating her for her silence, her weakness, her twisted, unseen motives. She watched me quietly as I threw things, shrieking and crying out my fury. For the first time in the six months since her maiming, the crooked, lopsided smile faded from Chelsea's face.

"I thought you understood." Her words were ponderous, calm, sliding past her now-deformed lips. The marks which diluted their natural shape had faded into a livid pink.

"Understand? How could I understand! You never told me why; I thought we were best friends! I thought we were close!"

"I thought you would understand. We were alike. We cared so much about what people thought. We cared about being pretty, popular. We were weak."

The conviction in her voice stopped me cold. "Weak?"

It was back on her face now, that twisted smile. "Yes, we were weak. Now I'm strong." She fondled her smooth, hairless arm. "It's the toughest tissue in the body. Nobody can hurt me anymore. I'm invincible." The light in her eyes wasn't manic or insane. Just . . . content.

I backed out the door, sick with horror, disgusted.

Before I got home, I called my roommate and asked her to hide all the knives. 𝄢

ILLUSTRATION BY THOMAS CHRISTOPH

THEY CAST SPELLS
AND THEY LAUGHED —
THEN THEY STOPPED LAUGHING

Night of the Imago Moon

by Kiel Stuart

H.P. LOVECRAFT'S MAGAZINE OF HORROR

O f course the girls would be going out; it was Halloween, and a Friday. But first, Faradice and Darci would try to contact the goddess Imago.

"Hey!" Darci rapped on the floor.

Startled, Farry blinked at the girl facing her, at the boy-cropped hair and fierce little body weighted down with silver jewelry. She thought: *Angry, sure, but we all are, right? Me, I'm always restless, itchy, exploding.*

Faradice's parents had split up the summer before. Neither one wanted her. She'd come to stay with Aunt Jeannette on Long Island. But reconciliation was not what she asked of the goddess.

"Would you come on!" Darci was simmering now.

"Sorry. What?"

"You're not chanting. Do I have to do this myself?" Without waiting, Darci began: *"'Arise! Awake! Imago take control of me,'"* and Farry hastily joined in:

``*That I may free the wish within*

``*My spirit's skin. For worship's sake, this plea I make."*

They stopped, gazing anxiously at the little copper statue of Imago, goddess of dreams, horned, bare-breasted, she of the four arms: Imago who gives, Imago who takes.

The statue continued to emit aromatic smoke, but that was merely the incense brazier in its base.

Darci scowled. "Ah, Hell, this isn't working." She got to her feet. "Come on. We might as well go meet the guys."

"Maybe she needs an offering," suggested Faradice.

"Then you do it!" Failure to summon the goddess had put Darci in a foul temper.

An offering, thought Faradice, Why not? Darci never told me what she wanted from Imago, but I know what I'd ask.

Faradice reached up and detached one of her tiny copper earrings into the still-smoking brazier at Imago's feet.

And a spark from the statue flew out. Ping! It landed on Faradice's hand. "Ow! Boy, that was weird." She glanced back to see if Darci had noticed, but the other girl had already gone.

Outside, the wind howled cold.

The boys were already waiting. Faradice glanced at the clouded moon. It was a storm-bead, an icy elegance drawing her toward a circle of copperish light.

She looked to see if Darci had noticed the moon too, but Darci charged ahead.

Faradice sighed. The kids who had taken her up never went to the city, never went clubbing, preferred instead to skulk close to home. Why?

You want me to wear black? she thought, *Fine. I'll wear black. Listen to Francois Couperin? I'll do that too. But I'll never be one of you, because I've been through this before and it doesn't work.*

The wind moaned in her ear. *Imago of the four arms,* she thought, *Wind and dark, cloud and moon: Did you grant what I wished?*

She knew what it was, but would never utter a word of it to anyone. It was more than her clothes: black on black like everyone else's. That costume had never felt right. A fairy princess, in silver and gold, with a dragon to ride. That was her dream. But speak it? Not in this crowd.

She hurried to catch up with Darci.

Two boys, one tall, one slight, lounged against an abandoned panel truck. Bram, the smaller one, sneered with his whole body. The hulking Verlaine was less easy to read, his body language slow and gentle, eyes lidded but not secretive, sex and danger glittering there.

"Well?" Bram sauntered forward. "Any goddess action?"

"Shut up," sulked Darci. "Let's see you do any better."

Bram shoved a glowing joint at Faradice; she wrinkled her nose at its pungent scent. Bram's pre-Goth name had been Johnny, but he had buried all vestiges of his former life under top hat, ruffled shirt, black nail polish, and white make-up. "What's the matter, Farry?" he said. "Afraid you'll catch something from us peasants?"

Verlaine pushed his big form between them. "Leave her alone, why don't you?"

Faradice smiled. It was rare for Verlaine to speak in complete sentences, and he was the only one not in the official garb, his jeans and jersey reminiscent of an earlier age.

Bram shrugged. "Fine. More for the rest of us."

Darci laughed, wrestling Bram for possession.

Suddenly Faradice needed to be alone, to breathe, to gaze up at Imago's twin-horned moon in peace. She turned and ran.

"Wait!" called Verlaine.

She kept running. She ran until she didn't know where she was. Even the houses looked different: not the usual Colonial and Cape Cod and ranch, but looking like some mad architect had slashed off pieces of different homes and slapped them back together at random.

Where am I?

The others were trying to catch up. The air tasted of copper and magic.

It was in front of a pile of leaves and compost that she stopped, body quivering like a tuning fork. Gasping from her run, she felt torn in four different directions.

Who am I? she wondered, *where do I fit?*

She clenched her fists, jerked her head back toward the Imago moon. A surge of raw power ripped through her, quite alien, catching her the way time seizes a lump of coal and crushes it to diamond.

The power of the goddess. It wounded, it was fire, a spear, it would split her in two.

She struggled against it a moment, but the force brushed her aside, and she shouted, in a voice not her own:

"Arise! Awake! Imago take control of thee
"That I may see thy wings unfurl, thy mighty swirl
"That splits the night from black to black!"

The echo died. The pile of leaves began to move as if something was hiding beneath it, turning it from dead olive to copper-gold.

The others caught up with her. "What the hell is this place?" wheezed Darci. "And these weird houses . . ."

"Ho-ly sh—" said Bram, and stopped.

The pile of leaves was becoming.

Then, like snapping off a light-switch, the pain was gone. Faradice gasped in relief. Then saw what was before her. The great mound of leaves was no more. Instead, a head, body, tail, wings. It opened emerald eyes and gazed upon her.

My dragon. Her heart leapt.

It lurched up on its claws, awkward as a newborn colt, the wings making it seem enormous. A flinty odor of thunderstorm air came swirling up. Its wings tore a wind through Faradice's clothes and hair.

Then it calmed, nosing its hesitant way toward her.

"Look out!" screamed Darci.

"We better figure out what's going on," said Bram.

"We?" She whirled, furious. Had they shared her pain? Then why should they share her creation? "This is my dragon! I made him! Not you! What did you want of the goddess anyway, what did you ask for?"

Darci and Bram exchanged glances.

Faradice nodded. "I thought so."

"You are one arrogant bitch, know that?" said Bram.

"Want to see how arrogant? The rest of you go back to your doping and groping. I'm out of here."

Verlaine reached for her. "Farry, please . . ."

The dragon flung up its copper-gold head and uttered a roar. Flame jetted from its nostrils.

The others scattered. Only Verlaine stood his ground.

The dragon's intelligence was feeling its way toward hers on fast-growing tendrils; she could sense it like words on the edge

of the ocean's seashell hum. And in this new mind lived image, sound, almost speech — and it grew stronger, and it *was* speech.

Fly, said the dragon.

Here, now? she thought back.

Yes.

She put a hand on the dragon's long neck, and swung up onto its back. Powerful muscles flexed beneath its skin. She tucked her knees firmly behind its wings.

Verlaine called out: "Farry, careful!"

Away, away! she thought to the dragon, and it — he! — broke into a rough canter, then sprang into the air. Faradice gasped. The rush of his wings echoed her heartbeats. Air slapped her face as they climbed. She spared a single glance below. The others were running now, as if trying to catch her. She laughed; wind tore the sound away.

I'll call you Firewing, she told the dragon.

The land below them was a gameboard, pierced by the faraway glitter of Lake Ronkonkoma. Then the glitter came rushing up, and with a gasp she realized they were going into the lake, she would drown, she would —

— Plash! They were swimming through water that hissed with the dragon's passage, startled fish scattering before them, and for one terrifying instant Faradice could not breathe and then —

— she heard strange sounds, almost voices, smelled scents of almost forgotten dreams and —

— Firewing exploded from the water. She gasped, struck with the rush of cold air, teeth chattering. She would freeze and break like an icicle, lose her grip, fall. But then a delicious warmth spread from Firewing's body to hers, as if she was sitting on a radiator. Steam rose smoking from her wet clothes. She lifted her hands in exhilaration.

I'm free, she thought. *Lands far away, palaces of ice and fire on distant worlds. Princess, clad in silver and gold.*

For a while they drifted in the sky, watched only by the Imago moon. She who gives, she who takes.

THEY HAD RIDDEN the skies for what seemed like hours when Faradice felt it. A sense, a tickling, a warning. There was danger, but not for her.

Curiously hyper-alert, as though someone far away had rung an alarm, she looked up at the moon.

Sketched against its surface was the goddess herself, proud and stern. An image flashed in Farry's mind.

The action was blurred at the edges, but the dramatis personae were clear enough: Darci and Bram and Verlaine, surrounded by a sea of blue air, standing still and cold.

Faradice looked down. She could no longer see the ground. There was instead a glowing blue fog that had not been there before, a patch of blue like the showpiece of a quilt.

Where are we? she wondered

This is your home, answered the dragon.

Something's wrong, said Farry, *and I must find out. Let me down just outside the fog, and wait in the sky. If you should come to harm I couldn't stand it.*

I am dragon. What harm can come to me? scoffed Firewing. But he did as she asked.

The fog, thick and swampish and real as a theatrical curtain. Cool air needled her skin. With a deep breath, she plunged inside the fog, blinked, looked around, got her bearings.

She was back among the strange stitched-together houses, alone, calling for her friends, her cries flat, muffled.

One single house, a structure she had not seen before, all black funhouse spires and buttresses.

Cautiously she inched forward to peer in one of the windows.

Inside, the house was a palace, shimmering in gold and marble, great sweeps of rooms that could not possibly be contained by one black house, no matter how large. Darci, Bram, Verlaine, stood side by side in the middle of a ballroom, still as statues, as if —

"Dead," she whispered, falling back from the window.

"Ah! There you are, child. Come with me."

Faradice whirled, heart hammering. Then she saw who it was, and breathed out in relief.

Help had arrived. It was a man. A man scarcely taller than she; well-spoken, clean, precise, the way you imagine rich people look and act. His hair, cropped short to reveal a balding head, was white shot through with black; a three-piece suit echoed the colors of his hair.

"My friends." She managed to gesture. "Help them."

"Of course." He extended a manicured hand. "Come."

She glanced at him. "Where?"

"Why, into my house."

She blinked in confusion.

"I am Jotham, your host. And the party would not be complete without you." He floated toward her.

"P-party?" She drew back, then froze, a rabbit caught in onrushing headlights.

Jotham. The pupils of his eyes sparked with red lights. He smiled: his lips slid apart, revealing the teeth of a shark. His tongue was blue.

Gooseflesh raked her arms. Jotham put out a hand, touched her with one fingertip. Her muscles melted, leaving her limp and obedient. She felt her body rise, float, follow Jotham's steering finger to the front door. It swung open.

Jotham floated her through the door, into the ballroom, among her friends who stood like museum pieces. She turned to face Jotham. "What are you going to do with us?"

"Oh, Miss Knox," said Jotham. He waved a languid hand toward the others. "Don't you see? Such a grand collection of souls. And I am so hungry."

Verlaine groaned, rubbed his eyes, reached out toward her. He shook his head sadly. "I thought you got away, at least."

"Me?" She gave a bitter laugh. "I was halfway to Jupiter."

"Why'd you come back?"

You, she thought. But she said nothing.

"Please be seated," said Jotham. "We will have tea."

A silver tea cart rolled around to each of them in turn.

Darci set her cup down. "A tea party? Is that all? I thought we were screwed for sure." She got up to wander around the ballroom, touching statues, paintings, ornaments. Smiling.

Bram flung himself sprawling into a velvet chair, one foot tapping a nervous jingle. Verlaine came to stand near Faradice. Her hand crept out toward his.

"Isn't this pleasant?" said Jotham.

If only he wouldn't smile, thought Faradice. "How did this happen, how did you —"

"Farry." Darci's voice cracked. She cleared her throat. "He got us when that dragon came to life."

Jotham rose. The tea tray hovered near him; he replaced his cup. "Let there be no error," he said. "A world exists alongside your own. You pass it every day but don't see it."

Bram lifted his lip. "So we have Little Miss Perfect and her stupid dragon to thank."

"Back off," growled Verlaine.

"However it came about," said Jotham, "I'm rather glad of this chance. By the way, Miss Knox, where is that dragon?"

"Where you can't get him," she murmured.

"Ah. But as I was saying. I was bored. Lonely." Jotham shut his eyes a moment.

"What would you want with a bunch like us?" Verlaine said. "What would anyone?"

Bram shrugged. "Who cares? I don't even believe in this anyway. I must be tripping out or something."

"Yes!" Jotham moved nearer to the boy and Farry watched, mesmerized. "That's what makes it such fun: you tell yourself this cannot possibly be. But let that not stand in our way."

Jotham reminded Farry of the men that she loved from old black-and-white films: Claude Rains, George Sanders. Graceful, mannered, gold-voiced.

He put one finger under Bram's chin and tipped the boy's face up toward his. "Let me tell you some things," purred Jotham. "This one is only afraid of the dark. He wants a kiss and a cuddle before bedtime. Isn't that true, Bram?"

Even the thick makeup could not conceal Bram's scarlet flush. "Fuck off."

"Dear boy," said Jotham, turning away. "Of course, little Darci is easy to explain. There is her love for fine things."

Darci had been stroking a marble dolphin.

"No, no, I think it's charming. We can become so attached to things. Can't we, dear? You don't mind them knowing you take a toy to bed with you, do you? I think it so refreshing in these days of childhood cynicism. A Raggedy Ann doll, I believe?"

Darci stood rigid, looking at the floor.

Jotham floated once around the room, his movements hypnotic. Faradice watched him with a sort of longing.

Jotham came to rest before Verlaine. The boy glared down at him. "Verlaine, our strong silent type, is less easy to categorize. But he fancies you, Miss Knox. Why, he thinks of nothing else. To the extent that, at night, when he is all alone, and under the covers, he takes one hand and —"

Verlaine paled. "Shut up!"

Jotham smiled, made another leisurely circle around the room. "But of course that leaves you."

"Don't try it," warned Verlaine.

Farry lifted her head. "No, Verlaine, it's all right. Everyone knows anyway. I'm a freak. Always on the outside looking in."

Jotham's hot-coal eyes caressed her for a moment. "Oh, but we are not speaking of that particular abnormality of yours." He turned away. "Did you children know that Miss Knox is a princess?"

This time it was her face that burned.

"A princess of the blood royal. Only fitting that this shall be her palace."

"Princess!" Bram sniggered. Even Darci giggled. Verlaine watched her with unreadable eyes.

"Isn't this pleasant? We will sit and talk and have tea. We will know each other better, much better. For this is only a start."

Faradice swallowed hard. "What do you mean?"

"You think those are your deepest secrets. Let me inform you, my dear, that there are secrets inside each of you that you

H. P. LOVECRAFT'S MAGAZINE OF HORROR

do not begin to suspect. It will be amusing to see if you survive learning them. And we have so much time."

"Why are you doing this?" she whispered.

He smiled, blue-tongued, beautiful, poisonous. "It is only what I am."

Of course. She knew what he was. She had grown up among such people. He would peck at their wounds, waiting until the wound skinned over, then peck again, never allowing any to fully heal. He would set them against one another, use their weaknesses, feast on their pain.

Too much like me, she thought.

She couldn't allow it to go on. She alone had reached Imago's power. She alone could stop him. The air darkened, turned blue with the grief of her choice.

She was ready. Again she called on Imago who gives, Imago who takes:

"Arise, awake!
"Imago take control of me
"That I might be
"The instrument to end this pain
"To counteract his venom rain."

"Stop what you're doing!" hissed Jotham. But Faradice tilted her head toward the Imago moon. She could not see it, but it answered, its cold power pouring through her, squeezing coal to diamond.

"I will not warn you again," said Jotham, but she could no longer respond. She felt her body liquefy, spin a chrysalis around itself. The tides of her blood churned, and for a split-second she was nowhere, nothing.

Then, *becoming.*

First the dragon intelligence. She was ichor and water, fire and smoke. Tree and night and wind and wisdom.

Then the change of bones and skin, the stretching and cracking. A plunge into water, a dizziment of tastes, sounds, scents. Steam. Billow. Green. Gold.

Heat. Unbearable heat.

The melding was complete. Her throat was hot with rage. She opened emerald eyes.

She let out the rage. A blast of flame jetted from her throat, knocked down one wall of the house. A dragon stood in gold and copper splendor, dangerous, powerful. A dragon faced Jotham, and uttered a roar of defiance and hope.

Jotham drew back his lips. "Even this will not save you. You are dead already. You were dead the moment you called on Imago. She gives. She takes."

Fire. The flames grew, rose in a ring around them. From far away she heard screams.

Jotham slid back his lips and spat a long tongue of blue poison that crossed her body like a freezing blade. In a spasm of pain she raised her wings, lashed out with her tail, knocked him aside. The flames rose in a wall of hot gold.

But the poison had done its work. As the house burned, as Jotham burned, she felt herself die.

Pulse slowing, freezing, congealing to ice. But as the poison spread to do its blue deed she felt astonishment. Not death but separation, a parting of the dragon intelligence, the peeling away of a bandage. No! She wanted to clutch him back to her, keep him safe, but his will was strong. The dragon rose from her body and looked back at her.

Go on, she heard.

But you'll die.

You heard Jotham. I'm dead anyway.

Please don't.

I owe my life to you. If Imago demands a sacrifice, then let it be this way.

Blink! They were outside the burning house, Darci and Bram weeping, clinging to one another, Verlaine literally holding her up. Blinking away smoke and tears, Faradice watched Jotham's house. Part of her was dying there. It burned a long time.

"Come on," whispered Verlaine. She leaned against his chest, inhaling his scent, allowing herself to relax for one beautiful moment in his arms. Then she let him steer her away. High above the four of them, the Imago moon looked down.

Faradice felt a hundred years old.

As they headed back toward safety, and the streets began to change into the streets they knew, Faradice understood that the goddess had given one last gift.

The first faint voices called out.

Every bush and tree leaned in to her, singing the resinous songs of wood and leaf. Then pale echoes of Firewing's voice came to her, voices of the little winged things, cousins to the dragon: cricket, bat, night bird, trilling inside her head, singing of choice and change, hot little insect voices, voices of inquiry and accusation, voices of sorrow and pain and regret, part of her now.

She would never stop hearing them. 𝄐

Kiel Stuart is a member of the Authors' Guild, SFWA, and HWA. Her poetry and fiction have appeared in many venues, including Weird Tales, Rough Beasts, *and* The Potomac Review. *She is a part-time filmmaker; and her mockumentary short, "Big Pants, Little Bikes," is now making the rounds of film festivals.*

"Night of the Imago Moon" came from a dream. Stuart specializes in portraying the struggle between the outsiders' need for acceptance and individuality.

Thinking of You

by Nicholas Knight

He didn't want to sit beside her. Well, actually he did, but he didn't want to scare her.

People are often jumpy at two A.M. in the subway station. Especially pretty young women alone in the presence of a man in a trench coat. It might be rewarding to startle her, though — see her chest heave. Cheap thrills for a wealthy man.

No, best to stop several feet away. He leaned against a plastic-encased movie poster that covered a large chunk of wall space. The poster advertised a supernatural horror film, but he paid it little attention. He thought such stories were for the simpleminded.

He stared at the woman, but she did not acknowledge him. She had to have sensed his approach, yet she didn't so much as glance his way.

He wondered what she was thinking about.

He fished in his pocket for a coin. "Penny for your thoughts," might make a decent icebreaker.

Though he didn't voice his thought aloud, she looked at him right then. And smiled.

There was something almost predatory about her smile.

No, just wishful thinking, he thought. Women didn't chase after him. At least not when they didn't know he was wealthy. And since his car was in the shop and his coat covered his suit, he knew he looked pretty plain.

She stood — gracefully, he thought — and walked over to him.

"I noticed you staring at me," she said.

"I, uh . . ."

"And I wondered what you were thinking." She held up a copper coin. "Penny for your thoughts?"

He knew it would sound lame to say he was thinking about how pretty she was, but that was the best line he could think of. Better than saying that he wanted to see her breathing heavy.

He reached for the penny, and said, "I was thinking about . . ." The soft touch of her hand momentarily distracted him. As he took the penny, his fingers received a mild electrical shock, which shot right up to his head and back again. He opened his mouth to continue what he'd been saying, but no words came out. He couldn't think of what he'd been thinking about. In fact he couldn't think of anything. She flashed her predatory smile again, and said, "Thank you for your thoughts." ᴳ

H. P. LOVECRAFT'S MAGAZINE OF HORROR

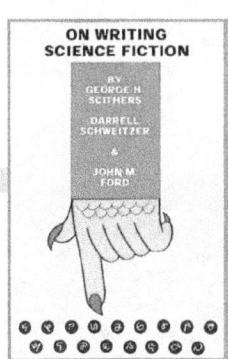

ILLUSTRATION BY STEPHEN COBURN

The Problem of the Missing Werewolf

by Ron Goulart

H arry Challenge didn't know he'd be encountering werewolves when he first undertook the case. He was anticipating a simple, routine bit of detective work.

He initially heard of Sir Duncan Motherwell by way of a cable-gram that found its way to him while he was dining in a quiet French restaurant near Covent Garden in London in the spring of 1900. The night outside was chill and the narrow cobbled street showing through the restaurant windows was thick with swirling, smoke-hued fog.

Sitting opposite Harry at the white-covered table was his portly magician friend, the Great Lorenzo. "Few people, other that a smattering of gifted adepts in far off Rangoon, have succeeded in mastering the art of teleportation," said Lorenzo, clapping his hands.

Accompanied by a puff of thick green smoke, a chocolate éclair appeared upon his previously empty dessert plate.

As Lorenzo picked up the éclair and took a generous bite, he added, "I am one of the few mystics outside of Rangoon and environs who can success-fully — "

"I saw you palm that off the dessert cart as you came in," mentioned Harry. He picked up his coffee cup.

"Still, my boy, you have to admit that it's an impressive illusion."

"What's really impressive is how you managed to keep that pastry from getting squashed throughout our meal."

"Alas, I can't reveal the secrets of my wizardry even to close chums such as . . . such as . . . " Setting down the half-eaten confection, the plump magician bent forward, groaning.

"You really have to cut down on the sweet stuff, Lorenzo."

Straightening up, grimacing, the Great Lorenzo said, his usually deep voice somewhat fluting, "This isn't indigestion, Harry." With a sigh, he leaned back in his chair. "Knowing me as you do, you're aware that, unless I'm in a patter mood, I make no claims to possessing true magical powers. Yet now and then, I'm visited with a vision that, though often slightly skewed, does indeed predict the future. I have just had one of those uninvited visions."

Harry nodded. "Some of them have had to do with me. Does this one?"

"It does indeed." The magician lifted the crisp napkin off his knee to wipe his now-perspiring face. "I saw, fleetingly, you being pursued through a fog-shrouded forest grove by a huge meanminded grey wolf. The slavering beast knocked you to the fetid ground, proceeding to sink his bloody fangs into your throat." Sighing again, he dropped his crumpled napkin on the table. Absently reaching beneath it, he produced a single yellow rose. "Excuse me, force of habit."

"That's all you saw?"

"It is, in all its grim entirety, my boy."

Taking out a thin, dark cigar, Harry unwrapped it. "Most of your brief glimpses of the future are never 100 percent accurate," he reminded as he lit the stogie.

"True, yet they've proved valuable on past occasions," countered Lorenzo. "As a generalized warning, if nothing else."

"Okay, I'll be very careful of any slavering grey wolves who come anywhere near me." He exhaled smoke. "Right now I'm between cases, so the chances of — "

"Scoff, Harry, yet keep in mind that — "

"M. Challenge?" Their waiter, a gaunt man in evening clothes that no longer fit him snugly, had stopped beside their table. On the silver salver he held in his gloved right hand rested a cablegram. "A boy just rushed this over from your hotel. I've reimbursed the lad."

"Thanks." Taking up the message, Harry dropped a coin on the plate.

"A message from your dear father in far off Manhattan," guessed Lorenzo.

"Seems so." Harry used a table knife to slit the envelope.

The message read—Dear Son: Enough London carousing with mountebanks, charlatans and magicians. Get yourself to Nightbridge Manor near village of Luddington in Barsetshire. Rich old coot named of Sir Duncan Motherwell has a simple missing person case for you. Cinch job, big fee. Move. Your loving father, the Challenge International Detective Agency.

Harry handed the message across to his plump friend. "A new case, but no wolves in the offing." He blew a small cloud of smoke toward the ceiling.

Frowning, the magician fluffed his prominent sideburns with his free hand. "I note he gave me third billing after mountebanks and charlatans," he observed, rattling the cablegram. "Even so, Harry, be on the lookout for ravenous beasts. You might also strive to avoid dangerous women."

"I always do," Harry assured him.

Harry's rooms at the Black Unicorn Inn in the village of Luddington were supplied with a plentitude of formidable furniture. The parlour, where he sat smoking as the massive grandfather clock in a shadowy corner struck midnight, was packed with an abundance of items.

There included a rush-seated settee, wicker revolving bookcase filled chiefly with bound volumes of Punch from the years 1876 through 1882 inclusive, a candy-striped loveseat, two bamboo end tables, two mismatched Morris chairs, a Chinese screen and a bentwood rocker.

Harry was sitting in the rocker going over the notes he'd made on his client before leaving London. A widower, Motherwell had amassed a considerable fortune with his Motherwell Pottery Company in the Five Towns and, after his knighthood five years ago, had purchased the venerable Nightbridge Manor in Barsetshire. Comfortably retired, he lived there with a half dozen servants and his daughter, who was twenty-two. Her name was Vesta and she was said to be outspoken and a bit of a New Woman.

The light rain that was falling when Harry checked into the Black Unicorn an hour earlier had increased to a heavy downpour. Lightning crackled in the woodlands behind the sprawling inn, thunder rumbled.

Because the ancient shutters guarding the parlour windows were being profoundly rattled by the night wind, Harry didn't at first notice the gentle knocking on his door.

Finally aware that someone was tapping timidly, he dropped his black-covered notebook on a bamboo table and stood. He patted his shoulder holster, then crossed to the heavy oaken door to open it a careful few inches.

A pale blonde young woman stood in the dimlit hallway. She wore a puff-sleeved blouse and a dark, full-length skirt. Touching at her rimless spectacles, she said in a small, prim voice. "Forgive me for disturbing you at such a late hour, Mr. Challenge — I am correct, am I not, in assuming that you are Harry Challenge, the noted inquiry agent?"

"I am, yeah, and what exactly — "

"In my desperation, sir, I am hoping you can help me with — "

"Sure, drop around first thing in the morning and — "

"Alas, I fear," she informed him as she commenced shivering, "that I may well not be alive by morning."

"Oh, so?"

"Might I, and do forgive my audacity, step inside for a few moments to explain my dilemma?"

"Sure." He opened the door wider, stepping back. "Come on in, Miss...?"

"Dear me, wherever are my manners?" She, cautiously and timidly, entered his cluttered parlour. "I'm Emily Whyte-Melville, a governess. It's about my latest employment that I wish to — "

"How'd you know who I was?"

Emily smiled, briefly and mildly. "Why, you're very well known in England, Mr. Challenge. Many's the time I've seen

your picture in exciting newspaper accounts of your detective exploits in England and on the Continent, many of the more sensational of them from the pen of a female journalist named Jennie Barr."

"She's a friend of mine. How'd you know I was staying at this inn and in this room?"

"I chanced to be gazing from the window of my own parlour when the carriage delivered you here from the station," she answered. "The light from the landlord's lantern illuminated your face long enough to allow me to recognize you. I later asked him in which room you were residing."

"Moderately probable," Harry acknowledged.

The perplexed young woman produced a faint gasping noise, pressing the fingers of her left hand gently to her breast. "Am I to infer, sir, that you doubt some portion of my account?"

He shrugged one shoulder. "Really difficult, ma'am, to hide a gun, even a Derringer like yours, under a blouse like that."

In a bolder voice she said, "In that case, Challenge," and reached inside her silken blouse for the small weapon he'd noticed concealed under her arm.

"C'mon, you don't think you can outdraw me?" He bounded forward and slugged her handsomely on the chin.

"Not cricket," she murmured, eyeballs rolling upward. Sighing, she fell to the flowered carpet, nearly smacking into a fat footstool.

Crouching, Harry unbuttoned the unconscious young woman's blouse to extract the Derringer from her shoulder holster. He then borrowed the wire that was holding up a framed engraving of two waifs who were in the process of perishing in a snow storm and tied her wrists and ankles together.

Gathering up the spurious governess, he carried her into the bedroom and tossed her onto the brass bed. The mattress made a spong sound, wisps of dust came flickering up.

Shutting the door, Harry retrieved his cigar from the ashtray. It had gone out. "I'll turn her over to the nearest constable in the morning," he said to himself.

Just then the hall door came flapping open.

A tall, lean man of about forty strolled in, holding a .38 revolver in his right hand. He was wearing an Inverness cape and a checkered cap, puffing on a sturdy briar pipe. "Thank the lord I'm in time," he exclaimed with relief. "I have good reason to believe, Challenge, that you'll shortly be visited by the only daughter of the second most dangerous criminal mastermind in the known world!"

T he lean intruder, having shed cape and cap, was puffing on his pipe as he paced Harry's parlour, "Let me explain," he said while acrid smoke floated around his sunbrowned face. "According to information that reached us at Scotland Yard scant hours ago, this young woman — "

"You're from Scotland Yard?"

The man halted. "My card," he said, passing one to Harry. "I am Inspector Sexton Beggarstaff of the International Conspiracy Division of the Yard."

Settling into one of the Morris chairs, Harry inquired, "Any relation to Sir Ambrose Beggarstaff?"

"My uncle, yes. Brilliant chap, though far too sedentary," replied the inspector. "I understand the old boy pulled your chestnuts out of the fire recently by helping you solve a case that had you utterly stumped."

"He exaggerates, but he did supply a few helpful hints."

Inspector Beggarstaff relit his pipe. "These are restless times, Challenge, a new century is about to dawn. Wars and revolutions multiply," he said. "In addition, many secret organizations have come into being, bent on world domination. Everyone has heard of the Camorra and the Si Fan, but for the past year and a half, ever since I was urgently recalled from Cairo, I've been on the trail of a sinister organization so secret that no one knows its true name."

"Boy, that is secret."

"At the Yard, we refer to it only as the Secret Society With No Name," continued the detective. "However, I have learned that it is an enormous worldwide union of insidious criminals and ruthless revolutionaries. Based in England, it is headed by a man known as Dr. Grimshaw, a criminal genius of impressive intelligence and gifted in numerous sciences, plus sorcery and alchemy. To those in his inner circle as well as to his mindless followers he is often referred to as the Devil Doctor."

"I've run into Grimshaw, but I thought he was currently locked away in Dartmoor Prison."

"Unfortunately no. Dr. Grimshaw escaped several months ago and is, I can assure you, back in business with a vengeance."

Harry asked the Scotland Yard man, "What exactly does all this have to do with me?"

Though Beggarstaff's pipe had gone out again, he continued to puff at it. "An astute question, and one I'd expect from a fellow detective of your reputation," he said. "We are fairly certain, Challenge, that the Devil Doctor has sent his only daughter, a beguiling young woman named Inza Grimshaw, to waylay you. Stunningly beautiful, astonishingly immoral, she is quite possibly one of the most dangerous women in Europe. And a master of disguise."

Harry pointed his thumb at the closed bedroom door. "She

must be the lady I decked a few minutes ago. You'll find her trussed up in there."

"Good lord!" Inspector Beggarstaff sprinted to the door, yanked it open and went diving into the bedroom.

Harry, after starting a fresh stogie, rose and followed in the wake of the inspector.

"The woman is devilishly clever." Beggarstaff turned up the oil lamp on the clawfooted bedside table, then indicated the tangle of wire that lay atop the empty bed. "She's eluded me yet again."

Harry shook his head. "And those were knots I learned from a Providence whaler in my youth."

"Inza Grimshaw, I can assure you, laughs at knots and manacles." The inspector strode to the half open window. "After slipping her bonds, the young lady bolted out of your window. It's only a twelve foot drop to the ground."

"Very gifted girl," agreed Harry. "Tell me why she wanted to divert me."

"I'm convinced it has something to do with Sir Duncan Motherwell."

"I'm supposed to see Motherwell in the morning about a simple missing persons case. How would that interest one of the world's top villains and his meanminded daughter?"

"I fear this Motherwell affair involves far more, Challenge." Beggarstaff took a folded message from an inner pocket of his Norfolk jacket. "This news was waiting for me when I arrived at the Luddington station." He cleared his throat. "Soon after dinner this evening, while putting out nuts for the squirrels in his wooded acres, Sir Duncan was attacked by what has been described as a large grey wolf. He lies in serious condition at Nightbridge Manor as we speak."

Early the next morning, having avoided Inspector Beggarstaff, Harry set out alone on horseback for Nightbridge Manor. The estate of his injured client lay roughly five miles north of the Black Unicorn. A trail through the forest acres led directly there.

A young woman came walking briskly over to Harry as he was turning his borrowed horse over to a Nightbridge stable boy. "The Challenge International Detective Agency is most certainly not living up to its reputation," she observed disdainfully. She was handsome and dark-haired, dressed in a riding habit. In her early twenties, she was nearly as tall as Harry and wore her long hair pulled back in a bun. "Had you arrived promptly, you might have saved my poor father from being attacked by a gigantic hound."

Harry leaned slightly, scanning her boots. Straightening, he eyed her outfit and her hair. "Nope, it's not a disguise."

"Of course it isn't and what in the bloody devil does that have to do with the matter at hand?"

"Not a damn thing, Miss Motherwell," he replied, grinning. "It's just that I'm in a cautious mood. What I was hired for, by the way, was to locate a missing person and not to protect your dad from big dogs."

Making an exasperated sound, Vesta Motherwell headed off toward the vast darkstone manor house, which lay a quarter mile uphill from the stables. "If you were any sort of competent

detective, you'd have realized that everything that's happened is inexorably linked."

Catching up with the rapidly striding Vesta, Harry asked, ""Everything being what?"

"My idiotic cousin's disappearance, the stolen manuscript and the vicious attack upon my father," she told him, rapidly and impatiently. "All these wretched events are connected. As you well ought to have deduced long ago, Mr. Challenge."

"Maybe you could provide a bit of information," he suggested as the young woman started determinedly up the broad red brick steps of the manor house. "For instance, what's your missing cousin's name?"

THE TURNER LANDSCAPE that had been wrenched from the study wall, gilt frame and all, was still lying on the Persian carpet. The door of the wall safe the painting had hidden hung open and the safe itself contained nothing but shadows.

"What do you make of this, Mr. Challenge?" asked Vesta.

"Offhand, ma'am, I'd venture to guess your father's safe had been looted."

"Of course it has," she said, angry. "I was hoping you'd give us some insight into who the cracksman was."

"A barefoot woman," he replied, unwrapping a new cheroot.

"Don't smoke that foul thing indoors, if you please," she warned him. "Are you being facetious about the identity of the thief?"

Putting the cigar away, he pointed a thumb in the direction of the French windows they'd just entered by. "One faint muddy footprint is peeking out from behind that drape on the left," he said, wandering over to the plush purple drape in question. "And on the backside of it, a place where she'd wiped her feet. Hence no more prints on your carpet."

"That fool Constable MacQuarrie didn't even notice that."

"Proving it pays to call in the Challenge Agency."

Kneeling, the young woman studied the single faint footprint. "But who is she?"

"I'll find out," promised Harry, settling into a leather armchair. "Tell me some more about your missing cousin and his stolen papers."

"I've already explained to you that my silly ass cousin, Avery Motherwell, fancies himself a gifted graphic artist. Nearly a year ago, he and a group of his decadent friends managed to scrape together enough funds to launch a wretched monthly satirical magazine that they christened *Piccadilly.*"

"I've seen it at railroad magazine stands."

"A fitting spot for such a wretched and irreverent periodical." She frowned in his direction. "Some months ago Avery fell in with some reckless and dissolute young people who dabble in both drugs and occult nonsense."

"And?"

"Last month he turned over to his attorneys a notebook and some random pages of a manuscript." His client's daughter leaned her backside against a section of dark-paneled wall. "They were instructed that should my cousin pass away, disappear or fail to contact them once a week, they were to convey his papers to my father — under guard to guarantee safe delivery."

"That's what was stowed in this safe?"

"Exactly."

"Okay, so what did Avery write about in those papers?"

"Errant nonsense," answered Vesta. "The few rambling pages I perused convinced me that what my cousin had produced was simply a work of deplorable fiction in the manner of such cheap novelists as H. Rider Haggard and H.G. Wells."

"Your father believed otherwise."

"My poor befuddled parent, yes, was convinced that every word was true," she answered. "Perhaps the sensational title Avery had appended to his unfinished manuscript misled my father. It was *Confessions of an English Lycanthrope.*"

Standing, Harry crossed to the French windows. "Your cousin claimed to be a werewolf?"

"The narrator of his penny dreadful manuscript maintained that he had joined a secret society," she said. "One of the diabolic tricks he acquired was the ability to turn himself into a large grey wolf whenever— "

"A large grey wolf like the one who attacked your father?"

Vesta came striding over to stand close to him. "You're drawing a foolish conclusion. My father was savaged by a wild dog," he asserted. "There are several of them roaming the woodlands."

He grinned. "And this wild dog opened the safe as well?"

"For a professional investigator, Mr. Challenge, you jump to conclusions as recklessly as our wooly-headed Inspector MacQuarrie."

"If your cousin's papers only represent an attempt to grind out a potboiler, then why were they delivered to Sir Duncan under guard? More importantly, why were they swiped?"

Folding her arms, Vesta turned away from him. "I have no idea."

"Did this manuscript mention any names?"

"I only glanced at a few pages," she reminded him. "The narrator did say he was recruited into this secret organization by someone he'd met at a place near the London waterfront called the Mirabilis Club."

"That's a real place in London, a hangout for — "

"Many a work of fiction refers to real locations."

"Let's move on to the question of where your missing cousin has gotten to. "Harry returned to the leather chair. "Any notions about — "

There was a knock on the study door.

"That must be Dr. Needham," said the young woman. "Come in."

The door opened and a bearded man in a rumpled tweed suit looked in. "I'm most sorry to interrupt you, Miss Motherwell," he said. "But your father is feeling a bit better and would like very much to converse with Mr. Challenge." He nodded at Harry. "I assume you're Mr. Challenge."

"That's me, yep."

"Father will only try to fill your head with a lot of rubbish," warned Vesta.

"As long as we've been paid our fee, I'll listen to anything." Harry followed the doctor into the hallway.

His client was covered nearly to his whiskered chin with a venerable multi-patterned patchwork quilt. His bald head had three sticking plasters slapped atop it, his puffy pink face showed several deep zigzag scratches and bruises. There was a wide bandage round his forehead, a smaller one covering most of his right ear.

Sir Duncan Motherwell, one bandaged hand taking hold of the edge of the quilt, used his other elbow to boost himself into a more upright position in the canopy bed. "Get your arse out of here," he suggested in a rumbling voice.

He was addressing not Harry but the rumpled doctor, who was hesitating on the threshold of the sick room. "I wanted to make certain that you don't strain — "

"Begone, you doddering quack."

"Don't cause him any stress, Mr. Challenge," cautioned the physician as he stepped back and, very quietly, shut the door.

"Damme, the man's a bloody fool," observed Motherwell. "You're a bit shorter than I anticipated, Challenge."

Harry crossed to the bedside. "All our taller operatives are busy."

His client made a sound that might have been a chuckle. "I appreciate a bit of humour," he acknowledged, "though I do not tolerate flippancy."

Harry grinned and asked, "What did you want to tell me?"

Sir Duncan scratched his bewhiskered uppermost chin. "It is my understanding that the Challenge organization has experience dealing with matters of an occult and supernatural nature."

Harry nodded. "Yeah, we handle a lot more than missing relatives."

"The situation has altered considerably since I communicated with your father," he older man told him. "I've been seriously mauled by a werewolf, which broadens the scope of your job."

Harry seated himself in a nearby bentwood chair. "You don't believe it was a big grey dog?"

"I can tell a blinking wolf from a mangy hound, sir."

"And a werewolf from a real wolf?"

"A real wolf would not have spoken to me just prior to

leaping at me out of the misty night," Motherwell informed him. "The damnable creature said, 'You know too much, Motherwell.' Then it leaped, knocking me arse over teakettle. Luckily I was able to, eventually, fend off the creature and escape with my life."

Leaning forward, Harry asked, "Does what you know too much about have to do with Avery Motherwell's missing papers?"

"That is my impression, sir," Sir Duncan replied. "At first I assumed that the papers were fragments of a wooly-headed attempt to write a scientific romance." He paused to inhale and exhale, slowly and wheezingly. "The fragments, however, could also be interpreted as a sort of confession of an addle-pated young wastrel who'd fallen into extremely bad company. Initially I was more concerned with Avery's whereabouts, since his jottings would not have been delivered to me had he not vanished."

"Now that you've been attacked, you believe he sent you a true account?"

"Precisely."

"Your daughter tells me you read every word of the stuff," said Harry. "So what do you remember of what Avery had to say?"

Sir Duncan told him.

Before he took his leave of the Nightbridge estate, Harry, alone, looked over the site of the werewolf attack.

At the woodland's edge he spotted Sir Duncan's footprints as well as the paw prints of a medium-size wolf. The mossy ground was churned up, speckles of blood dotted the brush.

Crouching slightly, he commenced following the traces of the wolf. The paw prints led him deeper into the forest. After about thirty yards the wolf tracks ceased, replaced by the prints of bare feet. They had been made by the small unshod feet of a young woman. "Looks to be the same lass who cracked the safe," Harry observed.

After pausing to light a cheroot, he started following the feminine footprints. These led him, after nearly five minutes, to the edge of a wide, green-surfaced forest pond.

Harry was about to begin circling the pond when a voice from his left said, "She put on a pair of hiking boots on the other side, old man. Then climbed up to the nearest roadway, departing in a waiting carriage. Impossible to trace thereafter, I'm afraid."

Turning, Harry tipped his bowler hat to Inspector Beggarstaff as the detective emerged from among the surrounding elms and beeches. "Which direction did she head?"

"North, toward the train station." The lean Scotland Yard man tugged out his tobacco pouch to fill his briar. "Since that's a well-traveled roadway, the tracks of her vehicle have long since been obliterated."

After puffing his cigar, Harry asked, "You think it was Inza Grimshaw?"

"As I've mentioned, Challenge, I'm damned certain we're dealing with the organization with no name here, the organization led by her father," answered the inspector. "It is quite pos-

sible that Inza herself attacked Sir Duncan and stole Avery Motherwell's notes."

"And then came back again to incapacitate me?"

"She's an audacious and dangerous creature."

"Well, I'll be wending my way back to the Black Unicorn."

After puffing thoughtfully on his pipe, Beggarstaff asked, "Did your interview with Sir Duncan supply any information on the werewolf attack?"

"Nothing you don't already know," lied Harry.

"I have the feeling, old man, that you're holding something back."

Harry spread his hands wide, assuming an honest-as-the-day-is-long expression. "Not at all, inspector," he assured him.

"VIRILITY?" SAID THE Great Lorenzo, who was leaning back against the padded leather seat of the bouncing carriage consuming the fat macaroon he'd just materialized out of thin air.

"According to the confessions of the disappearing Avery Motherwell, as recalled by his uncle, yeah," replied Harry. "Seems this Dr. Joshua Kling, successful inventor of Kling's All-Purpose Tonic, was trying to develop an elixir that would increase male stamina and staying power during romantic encounters."

"And instead he got a werewolf serum?"

Harry nodded.

Outside in the foggy London night the bell in an unseen church tower was sounding midnight. "That's a serious side effect." When the magician snapped his fingers, a bright multicolored feather duster appeared in his plump right hand. "The obliging duchess who loaned me this carriage frowns on crumbs on the upholstery."

"Some of the volunteers Dr. Kling tried the stuff out on only sprouted fur," continued Harry, looking out the carriage window at the thick mist. "But three others turned into large grey wolves."

"How long did they remain in such a state?" The Great Lorenzo dusted the carriage seat, his trousers and waistcoat and then his prominent side whiskers.

"The transition lasts from three to four hours, usually," said Harry. "To turn back into a wolf, you have to take another dose of the stuff. After Grimshaw persuaded Kling to work for him, they worked out a way for the serum users to switch back and forth between man and wolf at will. But that ability still only lasts for a few hours and then you need another dose."

"Apparently one of those early lupine volunteers mentioned the interesting effect of Dr. Kling's virility tonic to Dr. Grimshaw?"

"Yep, prompting Grimshaw to abduct Kling," answered Harry. "With a little persuasion, he got the doctor to cook up a batch of the serum. Grimshaw figured his unnamed society could put werewolves to good use."

"After being one of Grimshaw's werewolves for a while, Avery Motherwell got tired and tried to quit?"

"According to his uncle, Avery never sticks with anything for long." Harry eased closer to the open carriage window. "Think we're getting closer to the Thames."

Lorenzo tossed the feather duster toward the roof of the

compartment. It vanished. "I really think, my boy, that I should accompany you on — "

"Stop at the next corner," Harry called, leaning out the window.

"Soon as I can see it, sir," called the driver.

As the horse-drawn carriage rattled to a stop, Harry said to his friend, "Wait here, Lorenzo. Give me about a half an hour. Then if I don't come back, go fetch Inspector Beggarstaff from Scotland Yard."

"Be better if I go along with you, Harry."

"Nope." Harry eased out of the halted carriage and into the thick surrounding fog.

Next to the narrow-fronted three story Mirabilis Club, according to what Sir Duncan Motherwell had recalled of what he'd read in the now missing manuscript of his missing nephew, stood a deserted warehouse that once used to belong to the Soames International Tea Company.

Moving cautiously through the swirling midnight fog, Harry found the warehouse was exactly where it was supposed to be. As he used one of his lock picks on the venerable padlock on the weathered oaken door, he hoped that his client had remembered correctly what he'd read.

Once his eyes grew accustomed to the darkness inside the old warehouse, which still smelled strongly of an assortment of tea, especially Green Tea, Harry spotted the large japanned cabinet Sir Duncan had recalled.

As he eased closer to it, Harry said to himself, "And there are the two golden dragons on the doors." Shooting out his right hand, he poked his forefinger into the eye of the right side dragon.

The cabinet commenced shivering, producing a dim shaky rumbling. Slowly it began to swing out from the brick wall.

In less than five minutes a doorway-size opening showed in the wall.

Harry waited a moment before stepping across the threshold. From his pocket he withdrew his torch and clicked it on. A downward curving wooden stairway lay beyond the entryway.

Harry descended.

Some thirty-five feet down he reached a cobbled corridor. At its end two side passages branched off.

Halting, Harry listened.

From the darkness on his right came voices. Turning off his torch, Harry moved quietly into the blackness.

" . . . and you haven't read Ruskin?" an elderly man was saying.

"Never heard of him, old boy."

"Yet you call yourself an artist? I find that absolutely incredible." A sigh drifted along the corridor. "Ah, not only to be locked up in this foul hole, but to have to share it with an ill-educated gadabout who — "

"Easy now, I don't fancy being made sport of, you know. And I must say that your conversation hasn't been all that ruddy stimulating, doctor."

Harry saw a dim light coming from a barred cell about thirty feet along the stone passway. This was the dungeon area Avery's manuscript had mentioned.

"My dear young man — "

"It's not my fault you invented this bloody werewolf serum, don't you know. If you hadn't, I wouldn't have been turned into a blooming wolf and ordered to — "

"I was kidnapped, you young idiot. Forced to work for Dr. Grimshaw."

"Well, they ain't been trying to hypnotize you so you'd forget all about the goings on hereabouts, now have they?"

"Considering you have the brain capacity of a turnip, it's no wonder they haven't yet succeeded in successfully mesmerizing you."

"I say, that's a bit . . . Hello!" Avery Motherwell had noticed that Harry was standing just outside their cell.

"I'd advise quiet," suggested Harry, nodding at Dr. Joshua Kling and Motherwell.

"Who the dickens are you, old man? Not another bloody hypnotic Johnny?"

"Your uncle hired me to find you," Harry explained as he selected a pick to work on the cell door lock.

"Well, I say, that was white of the old boy." Avery was a pale, weedy young man, wearing a wrinkled, dusty Norfolk suit. "I'll just bet that Vesta didn't contribute to your fee. That girl fair loathes me, for no reason at all."

"I could suggest several highly plausible reasons for loathing you, young man," offered the stout, bearded Dr. Kling. "Sir, are you from Scotland Yard?"

"Nope, I'm Harry Challenge with the — "

"Challenge International Detective Agency," supplied the captive scientist. "Yes, I've heard of you. If you can convey me to Scotland Yard so that I may lodge a complaint against that scoundrel Dr. Grimshaw, I'd be most grateful, sir."

"You might think about tossing a few coppers his way, Doc," suggested Avery. "I mean to say, my Uncle Duncan hired this bloke to rescue me."

Hearing the lock click, Harry gently pulled the barred door open. Crossing the cell threshold, he asked the doctor, "Is Grimshaw still forcing you to work for him?"

Nodding, Kling answered, "I am of the opinion, sir, that the blackguard doesn't have anyone on his nefarious staff capable of producing fresh supplies of my virility serum. He long since forced me to give him the formula, yet he continues to put me to work producing more."

"That's hard cheese for you, Doc," put in Avery, frowning forlornly. "But my case is even worse. I mean to say, grabbed out of my bedchamber of an evening after I'd quietly resigned from Grimshaw's blinking organization and dragged into this foul — "

"Let us now," suggested Harry, moving toward the doorway, "get the hell out of here."

"Really, Challenge," said a female voice from out in the shadowy corridor, "you really didn't imagine you'd get out of here that easily, did you now?"

Inza Grimshaw, apparently undisguised, gestured with the .32 pearl-handled revolver in her gloved right hand. She was wearing a low-cut scarlet evening gown, a necklace of matched black pearls round her neck. "Get back into the cell," she urged Harry.

"You needn't have dressed up." He crossed into the stone room.

"I like to look my best at executions," Grimshaw's daughter told him, smiling. "Really you know, Challenge, you've been under observation ever since you opened the dragon door."

He shrugged. "Scotland Yard will be here in just about …" Casually he fished his heavy gold watch out of his vest pocket by its gilded chain. "Yeah, in just about ten minutes. Were I you folks, I'd be packing a portmanteau and heading for — "

"Oh, we'll be moving along," she said moving closer to him. "We'll be transporting Dr. Kling and this ninny Motherwell to a new location. You, however, the bobbies will find quite dead and done for on this very spot. Every since you trussed me up like a . . . Ow!"

Harry had swung the heavy watch at her gun hand. Inza's fingers snapped wide, the pistol falling free.

Shoving her and catching the weapon, Harry said, "Okay, ma'am, if you'll escort us out of here, we — "

"Fool!" She rubbed at a small pentagram that was tattooed on her left wrist, closing her eyes for a moment. "I'll destroy you."

The young woman began to shiver, at the same time seeming to diminish in size. The scarlet gown slid down her naked body, falling in a tangle on the floor of the cell. She dropped to all fours and then became a grey wolf, snarling at Harry.

He had the gun aimed at her. "Move and I'll shoot you," he warned.

"You need silver bullets to harm a werewolf," the animal taunted, readying to leap at him.

"Nope, actually that only applies to supernaturally produced wolves, Inza," he pointed out. "Scientifically produced wolves you can use any old bullets on."

Growling, the wolf leaped.

Harry dived to his left, firing at the creature as it sailed past him.

His shot took the wolf in the haunch.

The animal, bleeding, snarled and went rushing for the door.

They heard the wolf running along the corridor and then a loud splash.

"We're close to the Thames," said Dr. Kling. "And one of these tunnels leads there."

Avery was even paler. "Jove, but that was unpleasant to witness," he said. "I mean to say, when one turns into a shaggy beast oneself one doesn't see it from the same perspec — "

"We'll resume our departure," suggested Harry.

On a clear blue afternoon several days later, Harry was horseback riding in Rotten Row when he became aware that someone behind him was calling out to him. Slowing his white stallion, he glanced back,

Vesta Motherwell, mounted on a roan mare, was trotting in his wake. She was clad in a black riding habit. "You sit a horse surprisingly well for an American," she said as she moved up alongside him.

"Cowboys in the vicinity of Deadwood taught me in my youth. And how are you, Miss Motherwell?"

"A bit disgruntled," she acknowledged. "Father on the other hand is quite elated that you found poor Avery and that my cousin has given up, at least for now, some of his wastrel habits."

"At least he's no longer turning into a wolf."

"Yes, I am thankful for that, I suppose," the young woman admitted. "But while Avery is recuperating, he's residing with us at Nightbridge Manor. That's the reason I'm spending a few weeks in our London townhouse."

Harry nodded, saying nothing.

"I see by the accounts in the Times that Dr. Grimshaw's nefarious secret organization has broken up and he is believed to have fled England."

"For the moment."

As their horses trotted along the bridal path side by side, Vesta said, "But thanks to you he'll no longer have lycanthropy in his bag of tricks."

"True," replied Harry. "At least until he can find someone else to duplicate Kling's serum for him."

"It was unfortunate that Inza Grimshaw also escaped," said Vesta. "I assume that indicates that you possess a sentimental side when it comes to women outlaws and that you allowed her to get away."

"Actually, ma'am, I shot her in the rump," said Harry. "They left that detail out of most of the newspaper accounts."

"I see."

They rode on in silence for several moments.

"At any rate some of Dr. Grimshaw's minions were apprehended in the Scotland Yard raid of the Mirabilis Club."

"Minor minions, yeah."

"Will you be staying in London long?"

Harry answered, "Another week at least. My friend The Great Lorenzo plans to introduce a new trick in his magic show at the Royal Garden Theatre. He's calling it the Vanishing Wolf Illusion and I promised I'd drop in some performance to watch."

"That sounds most interesting," said Vesta. "Might I accompany you?"

"You might," said Harry. ᴦ

Ron Goulart has over 180 books to his credit, including more than 50 science fiction novels and more than 20 mystery novels. He has twice been nominated for an Edgar Award and is considered one of the country's leading authorities on comic books and comic strips. Ron lives with his wife Frances, also a writer, in Ridgefield, Connecticut.

Frightful Funnies

"OLD TOURIST HAUNT."

CARTOON BY MARC BILGREY